Squeeze Play

Squeeze Play

Jim Harrington

Dover and Blackstone Media L.L.C.
Pittsburgh, PA USA

Squeeze Play

Dover and Blackstone Media L.L.C.

For information address:
Dover and Blackstone Media L.L.C.
P.O. Box 12944
Pittsburgh, PA 15244-0944
www.doverandblackstone.com

ISBN: 978-0-9841160-0-3

Printed in the United States of America

Chapter One

The executioner glanced at his watch. If it was going to go down, it had to be soon—in a matter of minutes. Any longer and he'd miss his next "appointment." Then the victim appeared. The killer took a moment to size up his target. The man didn't seem special. He looked short, overweight, balding and either middle-aged or rapidly approaching that time in life. He seemed nervous and moved as though he expected something to happen. Of course, he was right.

He watched his victim walk down the opposite side of the street, stop at the corner, cross at the light and then walk to a newspaper stand. The killer crossed the street and stopped. His unsuspecting prey took a moment to buy a horse racing newspaper.

"Don't waste your money," the killer thought. "You're not gonna be around to read the first page."

He always fulfilled his contracts. He never missed. Never. He was the king of contract killing, a genuine superstar, the best in the business. Of course, the money was great, but it was the thrill that turned him on. The power, the danger, the hunt—these were the reasons he excelled in this deadly occupation.

He slid his right hand into his coat pocket and gripped the handle of a small revolver. Adrenaline pumped into his system. His eyes darted back and forth, taking in the whole scene. He settled into a fast walk; anything quicker would attract attention. Was he being watched? Had someone zeroed in on him? Another quick look. There were several other people on the street, but no one cared about him. He was just another face in the crowd.

Five steps away, he tightened his grip on the gun.

Four steps, he pulled it from his pocket.

At three steps, he cocked the hammer.

Two steps left, he raised the barrel to the back of the man's head.

And from a step behind, he fired.

The man dropped to the ground, much like a heavy sack of potatoes would fall if you lost your grip. There was no stumbling, no preliminary weakening of the knees. Nothing like you'd see in the movies. Everything gave, and he was down. The bullet had crashed through his skull and raced into his brain. It was as if the victim had thrown a switch and turned off the lights. He was dead in a heartbeat.

The killer didn't miss a step. He just kept walking. Half a block away, he stepped into a busy department store and blended with the customers. He knew the layout of the store and walked directly through the men's department to a rest room in the back of the building. He tossed the gun into a trash container. Then, he moved to the sink and peeled off the fake mustache. He wrapped it in paper, dropped it into the toilet and flushed. He disposed of the Pirates baseball cap and driving gloves, combed his hair and reversed his jacket.

On his way out of the store, he stopped and bought a couple of dress shirts, a pair of Dockers and some aftershave. He had walked into the store an escaping murderer looking for a place to hide, and left, an average, run-of-the-mill customer.

Down the street a crowd had gathered around the dead man. In the distance could be heard the scream of an approaching siren. "An ambulance," the killer thought. There was already more than the normal number of police cars at the scene.

He was overcome by a morbid curiosity. He walked back to the crowd. An attractive young woman stood off to one side, surveying the situation.

The killer smiled and she politely smiled back.

"What's all the commotion?" he asked.

"I'm not really sure," she answered. "There's a man on the ground over there, in the middle of the sidewalk. I think he's hurt pretty bad."

"How'd it happen?"

"I don't know!"

There was a pause in the conversation and then he continued, "Why don't we just go over there and find out."

The killer and the bystander walked closer, as if they were old friends. They maneuvered through the crowd of people until they were just a few feet from the body. The victim was lying face down, in a pool of dark red blood.

"My God! Is he dead?" the young woman asked.

"I don't think so. I think I saw him move," a spectator volunteered.

The response startled the assassin. "He looks dead to me," he said.

"With that much of his head missing, he's dead." It was the voice of a policeman, standing just to the other side of the killer.

The murderer tried not to look relieved. "Wow! How'd it happen?"

The policeman took out handkerchief and wiped his mouth. "Damned if I know. He sure pissed off *somebody,* and from the looks of it, that somebody hired a professional."

The young woman seemed genuinely surprised. "You mean this is a gangland hit?"

The cop shrugged his shoulders. "Gangland, shmangland. Hell, just about anybody can hire a hit man these days. You don't have to be in the mob. You just have to know the right—or should I say, the *wrong* people."

The killer shook his head. "Too bad." If you were looking for it, you could detect a slight smile on his face.

The policeman shook open a plastic bag. "Given the choice, I'd rather slip away quietly, in my sleep."

And with that he went on his way, in search of evidence.

An ambulance screeched to a stop and the attendants hurried from the cab. They were greeted by an older detective, obviously the man in charge. "Relax guys! This one's long gone."

The driver was taking some equipment from a storage compartment. "Well, if you don't mind, we'll check anyway. We get paid to do this."

The two medics hurried past the detective.

"Hey, I was just trying to help."

The murderer was now standing near the detective. After a moment, the investigator realized that this stranger was staring at him, sizing him up.

"What's your problem?" he asked.

The killer smiled. "I was just thinking—I'm glad I'm not in your shoes."

"Oh really! Why's that?" the detective asked defensively.

"Because I'd hate to have to pick up after this mess."

The assassin tucked his package under his arm and walked away.

Chapter Two

Jack Kane was a retired New York City detective who had, gracefully, made the transition from city cop to private investigator. The thing that bothered him the most about his city job was the never-ending barrage of red tape. On his own, he had eliminated most of it. He could cut corners, skirt details and get directly to the heart of the problem. To quote an old movie expression, Kane "could cut to the chase," and he liked that.

Fortunately, Kane worked well on very little sleep because, when he worked, nothing else mattered. It had been this total dedication to work that had cost him his marriage and the love of his children.

He had tried to salvage the relationship, with his family. A year before the family unit dissolved, Kane scrapped together all of his savings, borrowed some from old friends, and purchased an old lakefront boat club, in a town twenty miles northeast of Hartford, Connecticut. All of his adult life, he had dreamed of owning a little place up in Connecticut. It wasn't until he had actually started working the business that he realized it wasn't for him. He had worked hard, but his heart wasn't in it. What did a retired New York City police detective know about banquets and catering? With the boat club, there were never any high points—never any moments of success. It started off badly and quickly went belly-up. From then on, he vowed never again to stray from his area of expertise.

As his law enforcement career had developed, so had his wife's hatred for his work. It had become a mistress that she couldn't fight or compete with. A week after the boat club closed, Kane went to New York, to look for a job. It was the last day he and his wife shared the same residence. When he returned, she and the children were gone. He had never felt such an empty world.

Kane unloaded the boat club, taking a financial bath in the process. He lived for a few months in a dismal motel, on the outskirts of Port Chester, New York. What he liked and what he could afford were two different things. After a long search, Kane found an old farmhouse in north Stratford, Connecticut that fit his budget. It was perfect. A small house with a postcard view, of the Housatonic River. It was perfect for a loner. He wanted privacy, room to think and a place to regroup. It wasn't until the marriage had disintegrated that he realized how much he had loved his wife. Her absence created a hole in his world that he'd never be able to completely refill.

His uniform, these days, consisted of a thin windbreaker, crumpled fishing hat and beat-up boat shoes. When he traveled, Kane either drove his prized '72 Cutlass, a machine he kept in immaculate condition, or he took public transportation. He'd never been a very social man. Now that he lived alone, he was even more reclusive. He seemed to enjoy dealing with people only on a professional level, as a private detective—probably because he felt comfortable and in control. He was a loner and had few good friends. He worked better that way.

Most of what he did now involved marital snooping—what husband was sleeping with what girlfriend; whose wife was romancing whose lover? It paid the bills, but was a long way from his days as a homicide detective, on the NYPD. He missed the big cases, the exciting action. Deep down inside he knew that all he would need is the right set of circumstances and he'd jump at the opportunity to get involved in a real mystery again.

One springtime morning, that opportunity leaped at him from the front page of the *New York Daily News.* There, staring back at him, bigger than life, was a picture of an old friend, Sheldon Kaplan. Kaplan, informant by trade, had lived most of his miserable life on the cutting edge, passing information about the bad guys to the good guys and about the good guys to the bad guys and trying to do so without getting his head blown off. It was a juggling act he had performed successfully for over a quarter of a century. Judging from the front-page article, his luck had run out, on a sidewalk in Pittsburgh

"What the hell was he doing in Pittsburgh?" he asked himself.

True, Kaplan had been a snitch most all of his adult life, but he was a likable sort of guy, not your stereotypical weasel. Kane knew that his funeral would be well attended, because Kaplan had made so many friends. One of those friends was Jack Kane. Theirs was an unorthodox friendship that had begun two decades earlier when Kane was still in uniform. He was in the process of arresting Kaplan and another man. As he was handcuffing Kaplan, the accomplice pulled an ice pick from his coat sleeve. Kaplan pushed Kane out of the way and took the brunt of the attack himself. The assailant's blade plunged deep into his own right lung. For the next week and a half, Kaplan lay hospitalized, just a breath away from death. Kane owed Kaplan. It was a debt. He had to find the answers.

But where do you begin when you have so little to work with? Pittsburgh? What's in Pittsburgh? Kane knew very little about this western Pennsylvanian city. The closest he'd been to Pittsburgh was the metropolitan airport, and that was only to change planes.

Had Kaplan moved to Pittsburgh? New York had been so much a part of his life; it was unlikely he would have abandoned it for good. All of his connections were in New York. Pittsburgh wasn't his territory! The Big Apple was his home ground. He had to be out there on business. Nobody vacations in Pittsburgh.

But what kind of business? Nothing Kaplan did was legal. Kaplan being in Pittsburgh seemed as out of place as the Pope being in Los Vegas. Could it be that he was trying to branch out? No. In the forest of crime, Kaplan was a shrub. He had a hard enough time making it in New York.

Kane remembered that Kaplan had a small office on 42nd street, just down the block from Grand Central Terminal. It wasn't much bigger than a coat closet, but it served its purpose as headquarters for Kaplan Importers.

"Importers my ass!" Kane thought, "The only kind of order he took was, 'How much, on what horse, in what race?'" But it was a place to start.

The trip from Stamford to midtown Manhattan took about an hour. As soon as he had stepped into the Grand Central main concourse, Kane knew he was home. "You can take the kid outta New York, but you can't take the New York outta the kid." he thought. Kane was no stranger to Kaplan's office. He had been there on numerous occasions, squeezing information from his favorite informant.

After a five-minute walk, Kane was standing in the lobby of the old office building. He checked the directory. There it was: "Kaplan Importers, 2nd floor, Rm. 205."

There are a number of nice office buildings in New York. This was not one of them. If the owners made a profit, it sure wasn't used for maintenance and upkeep. One look at the elevator and Kane remembered how shaky it was the last time he had used it. He decided to take the stairs.

Kane knew that the police would have searched Kaplan's office by now. The odds of him finding anything were slim. But maybe he'd get lucky. Maybe they didn't know Kaplan like he did. Maybe something that meant nothing to them would mean everything to him. Room 205 was at the very end of a poorly lit hall. The floor was quiet. It didn't take Kane long to realize why. All of the other offices were empty. It looked like the abandoned set from a 1940s detective movie. A "B" movie at that.

Of course, the door was locked, but jimmying it was simple. Kane was amazed at how neat the police search had been. Kaplan's things weren't thrown around the room, and nothing appeared ripped or broken. Kane continued to pan the room.

"Alright, smart guy, you're here. Now what?" he thought.

It took a second before the blinking light on Kaplan's answering machine caught Kane's attention. Messages on the machine? Surely they came in after the police made their search. But why would they have left the tape? It would have been one of the first things they would have taken with them. Kane rewound the tape. He pressed the "play" button. The first message was from one of Kaplan's girlfriends. It was nothing special. She wanted him to take her out for a "good time." It was the next message that got his attention. Kaplan's answering machine was the type that logged the date and time after every message. Her message was from the day before Kaplan was murdered. The police hadn't listened to the tape!

"Sloppy—very sloppy."

The caller's voice made Kane's skin crawl. It was Kaplan.

"Hello me! I'm in Pittsburgh. Well, I'm at the airport anyway. I don't know why the hell 'the man' wants to see me, but mine is not to question why, mine is to do or die."

Kaplan paused for a moment. "I don't mind the *doing* so much. It's the *dying* that I have a lot of problems with." Kaplan laughed nervously.

"With reason," thought Kane.

"No one this big has ever wanted to see me in person before. Pittsburgh! What a joke. You'd think he'd be based in New York or Chicago or someplace. Hey! At least I'll get a game outta the trip. Ah, the reason why I'm calling myself. Don't forget to send the alimony check to Betty when I get back. If it's late again, she'll kill me."

Kane shook his head. "Someone beat her to it."

Kaplan's voice became very serious. "And one more thing. If—if for some reason something happens to me while I'm here—ah, that's ridiculous. Well, I see my ride's arrived."

Then there was a dial tone. It was the last message on the machine, and it was made just two hours before he was shot. Kane took the cassette and put it in his coat pocket.

"Shelley, my friend, what the hell did you get yourself into?"

He rifled Kaplan's desk, but it was hardly worth the effort. All he found were pens, stationary and a couple of back issues of *Playboy.*

"The classics were never your bag, were they you old rascal?"

He didn't have to break into Kaplan's only filing cabinet. The lock hadn't worked in years. Kane knew that Kaplan would have memorized the important stuff. Paper left a potentially dangerous trail. Just as he was about to close the last drawer, something caught his attention.

"Well, what have we here?"

It was a Polaroid picture attached to an envelope. As he was about to tear it open, Kane heard the loud rattling of the elevator at the other end of the hall. He stopped and took a breath, hoping that all he would hear would be the muffled sound of the street traffic below and the fading noise from the elevator as it passed in search of another floor. He was immediately disappointed. The elevator stopped and someone was getting off. No! Make that a whole bunch of people were getting off.

"Oh boy! I'm getting too old for this," he said as he closed the drawer and stuffed the picture and envelope into his jacket pocket.

Kane looked around the room for an exit. There weren't many options. He could hide under the desk or go out the window onto the fire escape. What he heard next helped him make his decision.

"Alright, Stone. Which one is Kaplan's office?"

Stone! Kane recognized the name immediately. He hoped he was wrong, but he had a feeling it was Ron Stone, one of the NYPD's sleaziest homicide detectives. Stone believed that rules weren't just meant to be broken, they were to be ignored altogether. As for his companion, Kane put two and two together and came up with Lieutenant Oswald Rumpler, one of Stone's career role models. They traveled in a set. If you met one, the other was sure to be close behind.

Now Kane knew why the police hadn't discovered the answering machine tape. They hadn't searched Kaplan's office yet. If Stone found Kane, he'd get great pleasure out of making life miserable for him. They hadn't gotten along when Kane was on the force, and nothing had happened to improve the relationship since his departure.

The window in Kaplan's office looked as if it hadn't been opened in years. Whoever painted the room last hadn't bothered opening it, and a thin coat of paint had effectively bonded the window to the frame. The elevator doors closed. From the sound of the footsteps, there were other policemen with Stone and Rumpler. Kane could feel himself becoming desperate. Then he saw the letter opener on Kaplan's desk.

"It's a long shot, but it might work," Kane thought, as he retrieved the tool. He jammed it through the dried paint that sealed the window and traced it around the frame, separating the two for the first time in probably a quarter of a century. Kane's initial thought was that the room must have been warmer with the window painted shut because he had immediately felt a very noticeable draft burst through the uncovered space between the window and the frame.

The police were just outside the door now and, for some reason, they were taking their time making an entrance. Maybe they were looking for a key or they still weren't sure which office was Kaplan's. There weren't any names on the doors, only numbers. Then again, maybe they heard something or saw one of Kane's movements through the translucent glass in the door.

"No more questions," Kane thought.

He snapped the window lock to the right, took hold of the two old-style handles and pulled. The window stuck for a moment and then gave way. Quickly, Kane stepped out onto the fire escape. Although it was spring, it was an unseasonably cold day. The stiff wind created a wind-chill factor of about thirty degrees. His light jacket was no match for the penetrating elements. As he turned to close the window behind him, he heard the rattle from the lock on the door.

"Boy, if you guys had worked the Son of Sam case, Berkowitz would still be on the street," Kane thought, making reference to their speed.

He leaned on the window to shut it but it stuck again, and this time it didn't budge when he exerted more effort.

"Son of a bitch!" Kane whispered.

He looked across at the door. Stone, Rumpler and company would see him as soon as they walked into the room and that should have been five seconds ago. Still, the only things shaking were the lock on the door—and Kane.

"Maybe God loves me after all!" he thought as he leaned into the window again. This time it slammed shut, with a bang.

"Damn!" Kane said in a much louder voice.

He made one more quick glance at the door, expecting to see it shattered by an assaulting police. Nothing. With the window closed, he couldn't even hear the unlocking of the door.

"You guys must be deft! But I'm not about to stick around and check your hearing."

Kane moved down the escape with the agility of a young man. "Not bad for an old dog in his mid-forties."

In a matter of a few seconds, he was on the ground, down the alley, around a corner and gone.

* * * *

Rumpler was the first one into the room. He hit a light switch and then turned to Stone and smiled.

"What do you think?" Stone asked, as he, too, stepped into the office.

Rumpler motioned to the two other patrolmen. "Why don't you two speak to the building manager and anyone around here who might be able to tell us something about Kaplan."

The uniforms turned and did as they were instructed.

"Alright, let's see where we stand," Rumpler continued.

The two men were completely familiar with the office. They'd been there before. They knew precisely where the answering machine was. Stone popped open the cover.

"Bingo!" he said, with a smile.

"Good. Very, very good." Rumpler grinned.

"Can you believe it? If it wasn't for Kaplan's tape, we'd have had to come up with a much more difficult plan.

"It really did make things much simpler, didn't it?" Rumpler looked up toward the ceiling. "Thanks Kaplan, you slime ball, wherever you are."

"Should I make the call?" Stone said, reaching for the phone on Kaplan's desk.

"Yes." He grabbed Stone's wrist. "But not from here! All we need is a record of the call on this line."

Stone replaced the phone.

"Yeah, right. I don't know what I was thinking of. I saw one down the corner I can use."

Rumpler's smile broadened. "Tell them—we were glad to be of service."

Chapter Three

Argari was just finishing his dinner when his right-hand man Alonzo Toma entered the dining room. Toma could see by the look on Argari's face that he didn't like being disturbed.

"Hey, Boss! I know how you don't like talking shop over dinner, but you said you wanted to be told as soon as we heard something from New York."

Argari tossed his napkin on to the table and stood up.

"Yeah, I did, didn't I?"

He took a cigar from a small canister on the mantel, lit it, took a big drag and then exhaled the smoke. "Well what have you got?"

"Those two guys we have on the payroll said that Kane's on his way here now."

"How do they know?" Argari asked as he puffed on his cigar.

"They set him up or something. Apparently, this is what happened, when they made their first inspection of the office, they came across a message that Kaplan had left on his own answering machine."

Argari sat back down in his chair and tapped the cigar ash into his plate.

"Message! What kind of message?"

Toma walked to the other end of the table. "I guess Kaplan used to leave messages for himself on his own answering machine—you know, reminders, memos, that kinda stuff."

Argari leaned back in his chair. "What kinda stuff was so important on this message?"

"They said that he was calling his office from a phone booth at Greater Pitt."

Argari's eyes widened. "Hmm, he was here when he made the call! Had to be just a few hours before our friend took him out."

"The guys in New York said that the message was made an hour and fifty minutes before the hit."

"What'd he say?"

"Just that he was in Pittsburgh and he was surprised that you wanted to meet with him here."

Argari jumped out of his chair. "He mentioned me on the tape?"

Toma waved his hand.

"No, no. Relax, boss. Kaplan didn't mention you by name. He referred to you as 'the man.' He didn't mention anyone's name. If he had, the guys would've destroyed it."

There was a short pause, then Toma went on. "You know, Boss, aren't you overdoing this revenge thing just a bit? I mean, it's been over ten years now."

Argari became loud. "I don't care if it's been *fifty* years. Time is not important here. He must be punished. Thanks to that weasel Kaplan, Kane was waiting for my brother at that warehouse. My kid brother didn't have a chance. Did you know that one of Kane's slugs caught my poor brother in the face? The face! You know that, don't you?"

"I know, Boss."

Argari looked insane. "We couldn't even open the damn casket. Son of a bitch, we couldn't even say good-bye properly. I've waited a long time—too, long. I can't wait any longer. Kane's gotta go and he's gotta go *now!*"

Argari crushed out the cigar.

Toma smiled. "What a waste of a good cigar, Boss."

Argari had regained his composure. "I can afford them."

There wasn't a hint of humor in Argari's voice. He continued, "When is Kane's plane due in?"

"The guys were calling from Newark. They said he had just taken off. I would guess he'll be here in the next hour or so."

"Get someone out to the airport. Follow him. I wanna know what he's doing."

"I'll get right on it."

Toma walked to the door stopped and turned back to Argari. "Hey. Boss, I gotta ask you. Why didn't we just do them both in New York?"

Argari's eyes were cold and filled with hatred.

Toma continued, "We could've killed Kaplan anywhere. Why go to all this trouble?"

Argari walked over to a window, that offered a magnificent city view. "You ever see how a cat kills its prey?"

"Yeah, I guess I have. So what?"

"No, I mean have you ever *really* watched how they do it?"

Toma looked puzzled. "I'm afraid I'm losing you, Boss."

"Usually, when a cat corners its prey, be it a mouse or whatever, it spends a little time playing with it—you know, slapping it around as it tries desperately to escape. Well, in this case, I'm the cat and Kane's the mouse, and I'm gonna have a little fun with him before I take him out. Why Pittsburgh? Because I want him in unfamiliar territory. I want him lost. Right now he doesn't have a clue where to start. If what you say is true and he doesn't have any names, for all he knows Jimmy Hoffa could be 'the man.' He may as well come here and start looking in the phonebook."

"We gonna use the kid again?" Toma asked.

Argari turned away from the window and leaned against the sill. "I'm not sure yet. As you know, Alonzo my good friend, we've created more than just your average 'mechanic.' We've developed the consummate killing machine. He likes his work, and he's good at it—damn good at it. And what a cover. There's a fairly large waiting list of jobs for him to do. His time is big money for us. To be honest with you, I'm really thinking about doing this one myself."

Toma looked surprised.

"You, Boss? You haven't done something like this in years. You really think you should? I mean, you got a lot to lose."

Argari seemed to take offense. "What? You think I've lost it? You don't think I have the nerve anymore? It's like riding a bicycle, Alonzo. Once you learn how, you never forget. Besides, the kid's got enough on his mind."

"That's another thing, Boss. Don't you think this job you got him doing this weekend is too big for just one guy?"

Argari walked back to his chair at the table. "Chicago says that it has to be done this weekend. It'll be our last opportunity. Monday morning he'll be on the floor of the US Senate proposing—make that, *demanding* the reopening of the Kennedy assassination investigation. And he'll *demand* that all the government's secret files be open to the public. And make no mistake Alonzo, these are not the files they're already talking about opening. Those are just a smoke screen—something to pacify the masses. I mean the *real* hardcore secret files—the ones that'll put a lot of important people behind bars.

"This guy carries a lot of weight. When he talks, the public listens and, what's more important, they believe. We've tried everything short of killing him to keep him quiet, but nothing's worked. Now we've gotta kill him. We have no choice. If he's alive on Monday, he opens a Pandora's Box. We can't let that happen. It will incriminate too many important people. There'll be a lot of embarrassing questions asked.

"No. The kid's gotta do the good senator this weekend, and he's gotta do him by himself. The fewer people who know about this, the better. The kid's the best. I have every confidence in his ability."

Toma's personal relationship with Argari allowed him the freedom to continue his questioning. "Hey Boss, why don't the guys who initiated the whole thing in the first place—the big shots in their big government agencies—why don't they take care of the good senator?"

It was obvious that Argari didn't like this line of questioning, but he answered anyway. "Because those 'big government agencies' have changed a great deal since 1963. They're no longer in the assassination business. If one of the 'players' were to recommend this, they'd be all over him, like a bear on honey."

Suddenly, Argari's whole expression changed. "Hey, wait a minute! Wait—a—minute! I just got a world-class idea. This has got to be divine intervention."

Toma didn't know what to make of Argari's abrupt mood change. "You've really lost me! What the hell are you talking about?"

"You remember how they made Oswald the patsy? Instead of me taking Kane out, why don't I just do to him what they did to that asshole in Dallas? Let his brothers in blue nail him. Why, history will label him a freaking lunatic, a nut! It's genius! It's beautiful!"

Toma had known Argari for years, yet he was constantly surprised at the wild new criminal ideas the man came up with. "Whew, I don't know. If this is the same Jack Kane we went up against in New York, years back, he's not stupid. He'll be a hard man to set up. How do you plan on doing it?"

Argari was on a roll. He started to pace as the idea came together in his mind. "I'm not sure yet. I'll think of something."

The idea had engulfed him. "Hard, yes. Impossible—no. Remember, right now he's coming to town to find out who killed his lowlife friend. He doesn't know a soul. He's gonna have to start from ground zero. What's his main weakness?"

Toma was about to respond but Argari didn't wait. "Simple. He's gonna have to put his trust in a lot of strangers. We'll make sure that those strangers are *our* strangers. We'll spoon feed him with whatever information we want him to have."

Toma smiled. “You amaze me. You still want me to send someone out to the airport?”

“Yeah. Let’s begin at the airport.”

Chapter Four

It was a short flight from Newark to Pittsburgh. It seemed that Kane had just received his snack when the flight attendants hurried up the aisle to collect trays and tell everyone to straighten their seatbacks in preparation for landing. Kane had a window seat and was lucky enough to be on the side of the airplane that faced Pittsburgh. It was a beautiful, sunny afternoon and the city seemed to sparkle like a new bracelet.

Sure, Kane had heard about all the good things that had happened to Pittsburgh over the past quarter century—its extensive urban redevelopment, its transformation from the steel capital to the nation's third-largest corporate headquarters center—even its being named "America's Most Livable City" by Rand McNally. But in his mind, he still equated Pittsburgh to smoke-belching mills, large ladles of molten metal, filth and pollution.

True, he had never visited the area before, but his 1960 Westport High School freshmen civics class had spent an entire chapter on American industrial centers, and Pittsburgh had been at the top of the list. The teacher's dramatic description of the grimy steel workers and the powerful blast furnaces they worked—combined with his textbook's colorful pictures—had made an indelible impression on his mind. What he saw and what he imagined were in conflict.

"It'll probably look different on the ground," he thought.

It had been a nice flight. Kane had always loved flying. He didn't get a chance to do much of it anymore. In Vietnam, he had flown helicopters, and at one point had entertained the idea of being a commercial pilot. A disastrous crash toward the end of his tour of duty had shattered his confidence as a pilot. He recovered, but two of his crew had died.

Heavy enemy ground fire had destroyed his chopper's engine, and it plummeted from the sky like a ton of bricks. He remembered his copilot reaching over and grabbing his wrist just before the aircraft nosed into the ground. He also remembered having to pry off his companion's death grip so that he could escape the burning wreckage. Kane could never forget crawling through the twisted metal looking for an exit and suddenly spotting the frozen expression of amazement on the dead door-gunner's face. The airman was pinned against the wall by a large piece of jagged metal—the way a note is pinned to a corkboard. Kane thought how surprised what's-his-name looked. It appeared as if his last thought on earth was, "This can't be me! I can't be dead!"

"Oh, man, what *was* his name? How could I forget!"

Kane was awakened from his daydreaming by the screech from the big jet's landing gear as it made contact with the runway. It was the twenty-first century again. This was Pittsburgh, and he was here to find "Kappy's" killer. The dead crewman's name wasn't important right now.

The detective traveled light. A valet bag and small suitcase were his only luggage. He always shipped his pistol to himself at the hotel where he was registered via "Next Day Delivery."

As usual, getting off the plane took longer than the flight itself. Kane's plane had parked at the farthest gate from the main terminal, and there would be a long walk.

Kane was surprised at how fast he got his bags. Usually, when he traveled, he waited twenty minutes to a half-hour, but this time he had them in ten minutes.

"Ten minutes! You guys are getting better at this," he said with a smile to the baggage attendant.

The man looked up with a straight face and replied, "Today—maybe, tomorrow. Who knows?"

Just as Kane was about hail a taxi, a man approached. "Hey, pal! If you're looking for a cab, mine's just around the corner."

"You licensed?"

The stranger laughed. "Absolutely. What? You don't take me for a gypsy, do you?"

Kane considered him for a moment and then nodded his approval. "I guess you're okay. I don't see any bandanas and tambourines."

"Here, let me take those," the cabby said as he took Kane's bags.

So far the cabby was telling the truth. His cab *was* "just around the corner" and he did have what appeared to be, a license. Kane was suspicious by nature.

"Why me? How come you picked me out of the crowd?"

The cabby pulled away from the curb. "Just the luck of the draw, I guess. I was coming back from the men's room and I saw you standing there. You looked like you needed a ride. I probably could have picked someone else. For some reason, I picked you. I don't know! Hey, if you don't want to ride with me, I'll be glad to let you out."

The driver turned the cab into another parking space and stopped.

"No, no, no. Sometimes I'm too damned suspicious for my own good. It's getting so I can't tell the good guys from the bad guys anymore."

The cabby smiled and started to drive again. "You—you're a cop aren't you?"

"Used to be, a long time ago."

The driver turned onto the parkway that went from the front of the terminal directly into Pittsburgh. "You know what they say, Mister, once a cop always a cop."

Kane smiled. "Is that what *they* say? Sounds like you know *them* pretty well."

The cabby glanced at him in his rearview mirror. "May seem hard to believe, but I used to be a cop."

Kane laughed a little and shook his head. "Son of a bitch! We're everywhere!"

The driver laughed. "Like flies on manure. I take it, from your accent, you're not from Pittsburgh."

"You're right. I'm from New York."

"Yeah, but, that's not a New York accent."

Kane smiled again. This guy was sharp. "Very good. I'm not from New York, originally. I__"

The cabby interrupted, "Wait! Don't tell me. It's a—a—New England accent. A southern New England accent. Probably from around New Haven or thereabouts."

Kane gave him a polite round of applause.

"Very good. You're not totally right, but still, I'm impressed."

"Where did I go wrong?"

"Well, I grew up in a small town just outside of Fall River, Massachusetts—a place called Westport."

"Fall River. That's where Lizzie Borden wasted her parents, right?"

"To put it mildly."

The cabby continued, "You know that broad was a piece of work. She takes out her parents and then remains cool, calm and collected throughout the trial. Some people think she did it in the nude, too, so that she wouldn't get any blood on her clothing."

The driver's eyes were wide with interest. The case had always fascinated Kane, too.

"Yeah, I've heard that. Others think she took off her clothes and put on her father's overcoat—the one they found blood-soaked under his head."

"No kidding! I never heard that one."

"It was a hot August day. He wouldn't have been wearing a topcoat, yet they found his propped under his head on the couch."

"You mean he was using it as a pillow," the cabby said.

"Or the murderer wanted the police to think that. It's pretty smart, when you think about it. You go to the hall closet, find Pop's overcoat and you put it on. Then, using your trusty little hatchet, you hack your parents to death. The coat gets covered with blood, you roll it up in a nice little ball, shove it under Dad's crushed skull—which, of course, is already lying in a pool of warm blood. You take a quick bath, change into a clean dress, and you're none the worse for the wear."

The driver seemed amazed. "You know what?"

"What?" Kane responded.

"Sounds like a woman you wouldn't want to piss off."

The two men laugh together.

"You seem to know a lot about Miss Lizzie," the driver commented.

"Yeah, well it's always been a big thing in my family. You see, I come from a long line of cops. My grandfather was a lieutenant in Fall River, and before him, my great-grandfather. As a matter of fact, my great-grandfather was assigned to guard the Borden house the night of the murder."

* * * *

Traffic was light and they were now almost half way to the city. Kane looked over at the driver's chauffeur license. "Thomas Caputo! Well Tom, were you city, county or state?"

Caputo glanced out his side window. It was a sensitive subject. "Federal."

Kane could hardly believe Caputo's answer. "What? You were FBI?"

"Yup. From 1982 to 1998—sixteen glorious years."

There was a momentary silence.

It was Caputo's turn. "How 'bout you?"

"NYPD, for twenty years and change. How come you left the Bureau?"

"There was an opening at the cab company." He laughed.

Caputo looked in the mirror and could see that Kane felt bad that he asked. "Hey, relax. It's history. I don't mind telling you, I was accused of not following Bureau procedure when we apprehended two killers."

"And?"

"And as a result of my actions, one of them grabbed my service revolver and shot my partner dead. Shot me, too, but not before I got my partner's pistol. I nailed her before she could hit me again—right between the her pretty blue eyes."

"Her?"

Caputo laughed again. "Yeah.. Maybe it was Lizzie Borden reincarnated! You see, these two killers were husband and wife—you know—the family that slays together, stays together—that kinda thing. Anyway, the husband, who by the way was killed two months ago in Western Penn.—that's one of our big prisons, up the Ohio River—"

He paused, realizing something. "Up the Ohio River.. Up the river. Hey! Maybe that's where they got the term! Who knows? Where was I?"

Kane reminded him. "You were telling me about the husband."

"Oh yeah, this guy was one sick son of a bitch. He kidnaps this multimillionaire's thirteen-year-old-daughter, ransoms her for two million dollars, gets the money, rapes the kid and then kills her. What's more, we think the wife watched."

"What makes you think that?" Kane asked.

Caputo rolled his window down a little and spit, as if there were something sour in his mouth. "When we caught these creatures, besides finding most of the money, we found pictures."

"Pictures!"

"Yeah—of that sick 'mother' assaulting that child and then—killing her. Someone had to take the pictures, and she was his only accomplice."

Kane imagined the cruelty. "Wow!"

There was another pause.

"So, what procedure did you supposedly break?"

"The bitch was pregnant. She looked innocent—fragile—maternal."

Kane knew immediately. "You didn't cuff her, right?"

"You got it. If I had, Frank would be alive today and I'd be about ready to collect my twenty-year pension."

Caputo's look became cold. "You know what's incredible?"

"What?"

"She was seven months pregnant. The baby died. You'd think I'd feel lousy, right? Well, I don't. I figure any kid from those two could only have been the devil himself."

* * * *

Suddenly they were entering the Fort Pitt Tunnel, the gateway to the city. It surprised Kane.

"Hey, this is kinda like the Holland Tunnel."

"Sort of, except instead of going under tons of water, this cuts through tons of rock."

"I'd hate to have either of them fall on me."

"Me too!" Caputo agreed. "Hey, I never asked you. Where do you wanna go?"

"Police headquarters."

"You looking for a job? It's not as crazy as New York, but Pittsburgh's a great place to live."

"No, I'm not looking for a job. I'm here on business."

The driver left the tunnel and now was on the Fort Pitt Bridge. Kane couldn't believe the view.

"You've gotta be kidding! This can't be Pittsburgh! This is beautiful."

Caputo smiled. "We natives try to keep this a secret. We don't want the word to get around or everybody'll be moving here. This ain't the Pittsburgh of Andrew Carnegie or J.P. Morgan. The days of pollution and dirt are gone forever. Over the course of the last quarter century, Pittsburgh's gone from being the ugly duckling to the beautiful swan."

Kane approved of what he saw. "I guess so."

Caputo directed the car down the center ramp, toward downtown. "Business! I thought you were off the force!"

"I am. I'm on my own now."

"Oh, you're a PI. What are you working on?"

Kane looked at Caputo. "A murder."

Caputo continued, "One that happened here?"

"Yeah. Last week."

"Would I have read about it?"

"I guess so. A friend of mine got his head blown off on a sidewalk, in your fair city."

"Professional?"

"Oh, yeah. This guy was smooth. He would have made Lizzie Borden proud."

"Wait! I did read about that. The guy's name was Kaiden!"

Kane corrected Caputo's mistake. "Kaplan."

"Kaplan. Right. The paper said he had a rap sheet ten miles long."

Kane smiled. "Sheldon had a tendency to attract trouble, the way a magnet attracts metal."

"How come he meant so much to you?"

Kane shook his head. "What makes you think he meant a lot to me?"

"Well, the mere fact that you're here tells me something."

Kane had been leaning forward so that it would be easier to carry on the conversation. He slumped back in the seat.

"Let's just say that we were friends—good friends."

A minute or so went by before either of the men spoke. Caputo broke the ice. "I have a few friends at headquarters who might be able to help you out—you know, get around the red tape—that kinda thing."

Caputo had said the right two words—"red tape." Kane leaned forward again. "What kind of friends?"

The traffic had become heavy, forcing the cabby to slow to a crawl.

"Friends who remember the help I used to give them when I was with the Bureau. Guys who, when they hear the name Tom Caputo think 'law officer' not 'cab driver.'"

"What's the problem? Why all the traffic?" Kane asked, noticing the congestion.

"Problem!" Caputo grinned. "You a baseball fan?"

"Oh, these people are headed to a Pirates game."

Caputo waved his hand. "Not just any old Pirates game. They're going over to see Johnny Reece pitch."

Kane knew the name. "I've heard about that kid. Won twenty games last year, didn't he?"

"Twenty-two, to be precise. The kid's deadly. And right now, he's ahead of last year's pace. Some people think he'll win thirty, this season."

Kane was impressed. "The man with the golden arm."

Caputo looked in the rearview mirror. "You can say that again."

Chapter Five

After waiting over half an hour for Caputo to come out of his friend's office, Kane started to have second thoughts about letting the cab driver intercede for him at the police station. Kane walked over to the desk sergeant. "Excuse me."

The rotund policeman looked up from his paperwork.

"Yeah?"

"My friend Mr. Caputo—he's been in there for an awfully long time."

The cop could have cared less. "So?"

"So, what's going on?"

"Obviously, they're talking."

Kane always hated a smart mouth. "Well, I kinda figured that he hadn't been arrested," he replied sarcastically.

"Look, I'm busy here. You wanna audition for *Saturday Night Live*, you do it somewhere else."

Now Kane was angry. He leaned over the desk. "Sergeant, how long have you been on the force?"

The man looked a little intimidated. "Uh, seven years!" he said defensively.

"How many of those seven years, right behind this desk?"

"Four."

"And where were you before that?"

"I don't have to—"

"Just answer the question!"

"Upstairs—in records."

Kane withdrew from his confrontational posture. "I spent about a quarter of century on the New York Police Department—most of those years as a homicide detective. I worked with a lot of policemen. You might say I was a cop's cop. In all my time on the force, I don't think I ever ran into a smart ass like you. You should be proud! You stand alone. You're one of a kind."

The sergeant hesitated. Just as he was about to talk, the office door opened and Caputo motioned to Kane. "Sorry to keep you waiting. Had to explain some stuff. Come on in."

Kane turned to the desk sergeant, as he was about to enter into the office. "Have a nice day."

He turned toward Caputo and continued, in a lower voice, "The rude son of a bitch!"

Caputo was amused. "Sounds like you found a new friend."

"I hope that's not a sample of Pittsburgh hospitality."

The friend Caputo had been talking to was dressed in what appeared to be a medium-priced navy blue suit. As Kane entered the room, he got up from his chair and extended his hand. "Detective Kane, good to meet you. I'm Bob Lauder."

Kane accepted the greeting. "Detective Lauder. Good to meet you, too."

Caputo sat down in one of the side chairs. "Bob's the big gun here."

Kane took the chair at the opposite side of the desk, and Lauder sat down in his chair.

"Big gun! What have you been drinking Tommy? I'm just the poor shmuck they dumped all the responsibility on."

"Yeah, but that's why they pay you the big bucks."

Lauder turned to Kane. "Do you believe this guy?"

"Hey! We just met! You know him better than *I* do."

Lauder took an open pack of cigarettes from his shirt pocket. "I hope you don't mind. I know it's a nasty habit, but a man's gotta have *some* vices."

"Smoked them for twenty-five years," Kane said half-heartily. "Looking back, I'll be damned if I can figure out why. I never really liked them."

"Some people say it's oral gratification—you know, like a baby sucking on its mother's breast," he said as he lit the smoke.

"Except, cigarettes are easier to light," Caputo chimed in.

Lauder gave Caputo a wry smile. "You know, they probably bounced you out of the Bureau because of your lousy sense of humor."

Caputo pretended to be hurt. "Low blow! I would have expected more from you Bobby! Especially after all the nice things I said about you."

Lauder waved his hand. "Enough of the bullshit. Our guest didn't fly in from New York to hear us trade barbs, did you Mr. Kane?"

"Hardly," Kane agreed.

Lauder took a drag on his cigarette. "If what Tommy says is true, I'm not sure there's a helluva lot we can do for you."

Kane shifted uncomfortably in his chair. "Look, I know the file's still open on this and it's against regulations to discuss the details of an active case, but if you can give me anything—anything at all, I'd really appreciate it."

Lauder smiled through a cloud of smoke. "Well, you must be the luckiest PI on the East Coast. If this ding-dong over here says you're okay, then that's good enough for me. And hell, he's working with you and he's like one of the force."

Kane turned quickly to Caputo, but the former lawman, seeing Kane's reaction, jumped into the conversation. "Bob's gonna let us look at what they have, Jack. I'd say were damned lucky."

It was more than Kane imagined. "Uh, great! That's terrific! When?"

It was Lauder's turn. "How about right now?"

Lauder placed the cigarette on an ashtray, opened a desk drawer and took out a thin Manila folder. He folded over the front cover and handed it across to Kane.

"It's a quick read."

Kane spent the next couple of minutes reading through the file. It contained the basics. Who was murdered, where, what time, by what method, estimated time of death—the things Kane already knew, and nothing else.

Kane looked up at Lauder. "Kaplan's been cold for awhile now. This is all you've got?"

Lauder leaned back in his chair. "Mr. Kane—"

Kane interrupted. "Mr. Kane was my father. Please, call me Jack."

Lauder smiled and continued, "Jack, a stranger flies to our town, comes in from the airport, registers at one of our nicer hotels downtown, goes out for a walk, buys a copy of *The Racing Forum* and gets his head blown off! You have to admit Jack, he didn't give us much to work with."

"Who's working it?"

Caputo answered, "Bob's handling this investigation, personally. That's why you were able to look at the file."

Kane was looking at Caputo but directed his comment to Lauder. "Kaplan had to talk to somebody."

"What do you mean?" There was an edginess in his voice.

"I mean, someone had to know Kaplan would be standing on that street corner. His killer didn't just get lucky and bump into him on the street."

Lauder shook his head. "We didn't find a record of any calls being made from his hotel room. If he talked to someone, it was either in person or from a pay phone."

Caputo leaned forward. "They called all the cab companies. We keep records of all our fares. There were none that matched Kaplan's description."

Kane placed the file back on the lieutenant's desk. "He didn't come by cab."

Lauder looked interested. "How do you know?"

"Because there was someone at the airport to pick him up."

Caputo looked over at Lauder and then back to Kane. "What makes you say that?"

"He called his own answering machine when he arrived in Pittsburgh. I guess he felt something wasn't right. While he was in the process of leaving his message, his ride showed up, and he cut it short."

Lauder seemed disturbed. "How did you find out about this tape? I never heard anything from the New York City police."

Kane smiled. "I have friends. I have my ways. Suffice it to say that the information is legit."

Caputo went on. "Did he know the name of the person who picked him up?"

Kane turned to Caputo. "If he did, he didn't have time to record it."

Caputo reached over and picked up the file. "Have you got this tape, Jack?"

"What! You think I'm nuts? If I did, I'd never admit to it."

`Lauder was poker-faced. "It's evidence. You could be arrested for withholding evidence in a murder investigation. That's serious, Jack."

Kane stood up. "What tape? I don't know what tape you're talking about! If you can find that cassette on me—if you can prove that I'm withholding evidence in this case, I'll turn myself in. I'll slap the handcuffs on myself."

Lauder was looking across at Kane, trying to read his face. "If you haven't got the tape, how'd you know about this call?"

"I told you, I have friends."

"Well then, why didn't the NYPD tell us? What the hell are they hiding?"

"I never said that my friends were on the NYPD."

Lauder shook his head. "Look, this is getting confusing. I'd like for all of us to be on the same page."

Kane started for the door. "Thanks for your help, guys. If you need me, I'll be at the Hilton."

He picked up the bags he had left next to the door and walked out of the room.

Lauder looked over at Caputo. "Stay close to him!"

Chapter Six

Toma walked into Argari's study. His boss was seated in a large, comfortable-looking leather chair, reading a Jack Higgins mystery. His appearance was baronial. It was hard to imagine that under the expensive smoking jacket and silk pajamas, beat the heart of a merciless killer.

Toma spoke softly. "Ah, excuse me, Boss."

Argari looked up from his book. "You ever read Jack Higgins?" He showed Toma the front cover.

"The guy's great! Lotta action. Makes you feel like you're right there in the middle of it. God knows, that's where I love to be."

Toma smiled. "Hey, Mr. Argari, I don't need to read action books when I work for you. I get all the action I can handle."

Argari was pleased with Toma's response. "Good point. What have you got?"

Toma moved a few steps closer. "A couple of things. First, Kane's in town and he's staying at the Hilton. As a matter of fact, he's in his room right now."

"Very good. I take it he's being shadowed?"

"We've got him covered like a blanket. Secondly, and you're not gonna like this, the kid is here."

"Why? I didn't send for him!"

"He says that he wants to talk about this weekend's job."

"We've already done that. There's nothing to talk about. Tell him I'm busy, and the next time he wants to talk, make an appointment."

Toma took a deep breath. He knew this wasn't going to be easy. "You're sure, Boss?"

Argari looked back at his book. "Absolutely. Now, get outta here."

Toma left the room, and the silence of a library returned. Argari was a real fan of Higgins. He had read everything the man had written. It didn't take long before he was totally engrossed in his book again. The only noise in the room was the systematic ticking of a mantel clock. Without warning, his peace was interrupted by one loud clicking sound, and it didn't match the ticking of the clock. It was the noise a revolver made when the hammer was cocked. Instantly, Argari realized why it was so loud. The barrel of the weapon was against his right ear. The Higgins book slid off Argari's lap.

"You're good, you son of a bitch. You're very good."

"For a man with a .357 magnum bullet six inches from his brain, you're exceptionally calm. You know, if my finger twitches, you'll never have to clean out your ears again."

"You're a lot of things, but you're not stupid. I'm your breadbasket. The big money comes through me. You do me and you might as well do yourself, too."

The room was silent for a moment. The assailant seemed to be considering his options. "You have a point," he said softly, as he pulled the pistol away from Argari's head and uncocked it. "I thought that our relationship was beyond appointments, Argari."

Argari stood up and faced the kid. "What'd you do to Toma?"

The killer smiled. "No permanent damage. He'll be fine."

"I don't appreciate people barging into my house like this, Reece."

"To be quite honest with you, Argari, I don't care what you don't like. Our teacher-student days are long gone. There's nothing you can teach me anymore."

Argari walked to his desk and took a cigarette out of a gold case. "You're getting pretty cocky, in your old age, Johnny."

"Yeah, well today wasn't one of my better outings."

Argari smiled. "I saw the game on TV. You got shelled."

"Days like today make me very nasty, Argari. I don't like it when people jerk my chain."

Argari took a moment to light the cigarette. "No one's jerking your chain, Johnny—at least no one I know."

Suddenly, the study door burst open and a wild-eyed Toma stumbled in. His left hand pressed a blood-soaked handkerchief against his head, and his right hand clenched a .45.

"You bastard! You can't do this to me and get away with it."

He raised the pistol to fire, but Argari calmly stepped between the two men. Toma hesitated.

Argari turned to Reece.

"Johnny, I think you owe Mr. Toma an apology."

Reece started to laugh. Toma became furious.

"Get out of the way, Boss. This guy's asking for it."

"Johnny, if you don't apologize, I'm afraid I won't be able to stop Mr. Toma from—"

"Dying," Reece finished as he stepped to one side and pointed his Magnum directly at Toma.

Toma squeezed the trigger, but it simply clicked.

"You idiot. You don't think I'd leave you lying out there with a loaded gun do you? You might hurt someone," Reece said, with a smile.

Toma squeezed again—another click. He made a move toward the exit but Reece fired a warning shot into the door.

"Don't move."

Argari returned to his chair and took a puff on his cigarette. He didn't say a word. He simply looked on, as if he were watching a play.

Reece walked over to Toma and calmly stuck the barrel into the man's mouth. "So, you're pissed at me. Is that a fair assumption, Toma?"

Toma didn't say a word. He merely swallowed hard.

"Maybe you have a right to be pissed at me, but given your position, I'd suggest that you let bygones be bygones, wouldn't you? Now, let me warn you. If I release you and you make any move to retaliate, I will kill you. There'll be no contest. You will die. And that means, you'd better not try shooting me in the back when I walk to my car."

Reece's smile widened. "I've got eyes behind my head."

He withdrew the gun from Toma's mouth, took the empty pistol from the man's hand, stepped back a couple of steps and slid his weapon into its holster.

Argari clapped his hands. "Bravo! Bravo! Well done."

He got up from his chair and crushed the cigarette out in an ashtray on his desk. "Now, if the two of you are finished, I'd suggest you go clean yourself up, Alonzo."

He turned to Reece. "As for you—sit down." He pointed to the couch.

Reece kept smiling and did what he was told.

Toma left the room without saying another word. Argari knew that Toma would never forget the embarrassment. The man couldn't have risen to his position without being unbelievably good at being incredibly deadly.

Argari walked over to the door, examined the bullet hole with his hand, shoved the lock closed and turned back to Reece. "This door cost three thousand dollars."

"Put it on my tab."

"You enjoy taking chances, don't you Johnny?"

"It's what makes my work so much fun," Reece answered.

Argari gestured toward the door. "You know, he's not through. He's gonna do everything in his power to kill you. You may not believe this, but Alonzo's good. There's a chance he'll succeed."

Reece shook his head. "I wouldn't bet on it. I meant what I said. He'll get killed."

Argari walked back to his chair. "Well, that's Alonzo's problem, isn't it?"

"That's what I love about you, Mr. Argari. Your loyalty to your troops."

Argari became angered. "I've learned that it pays to be loyal to one person—me. At least I know I'll never disappoint myself. Now what the hell's your problem? What's so important that it couldn't wait until tomorrow?"

"I usually don't dwell on jobs that I've completed, but this Kaplan hit's been on my mind."

Argari took another cigarette. "I thought you wanted to talk about this weekend's assignment?"

"That's just it. I've got a feeling they're related."

Argari reached across the desk for his lighter. "What are you talking about? How could a hit as big as the one this weekend have anything to do with a shmuck like Kaplan?"

Reece put an arm up on the back of the couch. "That's what I was hoping you could tell me."

Argari took moment to light the cigarette. "Originally, they had nothing to do with each other. They weren't related. The Kaplan hit was for me—for personal reasons."

Reece was serious now. "Well, let me get to the point. When I read about this Kaplan fella in the paper, I couldn't figure out why anyone would want to take him out. He was too small, too insignificant. Then it hit me. This guy's bait. You're using him to get back at somebody or to draw somebody to you or something like that. Am I right?"

Argari took a drag on the cigarette. "Look Johnny, I've got a lot invested in you. I taught you not to think about your hits, just do them. These aren't *people.* They're assignments. It's like taking out the trash. Don't worry about the reasons, just do the job."

Reece was intense. "There's something you're not telling me. Killing the senator isn't a problem so long as that's all I have to worry about. But if I find out that you were holding out on me—well, needless to say, I'll be very, very angry."

Reece got up and walked to the door.

Argari stood and gave him a strange look. Reece noticed it and stopped. "What's your problem?"

"You like this stuff, don't you?"

"Love it."

"You'd rather do this than play baseball!"

"No taxes and a longer career," Reece answered.

"Something I've never been able to figure out."

"And that is?"

"Why would a professional athlete with your talent ever get into this line of work?"

"There's only one answer, Argari, my good man."

"What's that?"

"I'm crazy."

With that he turned, unlocked the door and left the room.

Argari took another slow drag on his cigarette. "Well, that much I knew."

Chapter Seven

Kane sipped a large orange juice in the hotel coffee shop as he examined the Polaroid picture and envelope he had found in Kaplan's office. When he'd stuck it into his coat pocket, he had hoped it would be important, a case breaker. But if it was, Kane was having a hard time figuring out why it was important. The Polaroid was a snapshot of a Pittsburgh Pirates baseball player signing autographs at Shea Stadium, and on the back of the picture Kaplan had written "May 9th—Santori Shooting—GCT platform." The envelope had two words scribbled on it: "Duplicate Set." Inside were four more pictures of a young guy talking with an older man next to a limousine. The gray-haired character looked familiar, but Kane didn't have a clue who the younger man was.

"You look deep in thought!"

Kane looked up. It was Caputo. "Shouldn't you be out at the airport making a living?" Kane asked.

Caputo pointed to an empty chair. "Do you mind?"

Kane shook his head and Caputo sat down. "I've been thinking about the Kaplan murder all night. I wanna help."

Caputo stopped a passing waitress and ordered some coffee. Kane slid the pictures into the envelope.

"Look, Caputo, I appreciate your interest, but I don't know you. One second I'm at the airport alone and the next second I'm in a car, talking to a stranger about my friend's case. It's not that I don't trust you, it's just that, I—don't trust you."

Caputo smiled, took a sip of coffee and continued, "Look, I'm a cop!"

"An ex-cop. At least that's what you say you are."

"You think I could've gained access to those files yesterday if I wasn't what I said I was?"

"Who knows? Many times things aren't what they appear to be."

"What? You think Bob Lauder was a fake? An actor, maybe? Come on, get serious. You're starting to sound like you've read too many detective stories."

Kane finished his juice. "Hey, maybe I have."

Caputo took another sip. "Kane, I'm on your side. You're looking at a poor old government employee who has been wronged and unjustly punished. I want to prove I'm still worth something."

Kane smiled. "Sounds like *you've* been watching too many soaps."

"Maybe *I* have."

Kane took the picture of the ballplayer from the envelope and cupped it in his hand, like a poker player covering his cards. "Tell me, who's number eleven on the Pirates?"

The question seemed to surprise Caputo. "I'm not sure! I love baseball but I'll be damned if I can remember the players' numbers. Wait a second."

Caputo walked over to the counter, took the complimentary *Pittsburgh Post-Gazette* and came back to the table. He flipped through it until he came to the right section and then scanned the page.

"Number eleven is—none other than—Johnny Reece."

"The pitcher!"

"You've got it."

Kane looked down at the picture and then tossed it across to Caputo.

"Yup! That's him. Where'd you get this?"

Kane waved off the question. "That's not important."

He took another picture from the envelope. "And the young guy in this picture—I take it he's Reece, too."

Caputo's eyes widened. "Yeah! And he's with—"

Kane finished the sentence. "I know. Argari! We go way back. At first, I didn't recognize him. He's gotten older, fatter, balder. But after I looked at the picture for a while there was no mistaking him. His eyes give him away. He could grow a beard, he could have plastic surgery, but I'd always recognize him by his eyes."

Caputo swallowed what was left of his coffee. "His eyes, huh?"

Kane retrieved the pictures, placed them back into the envelope and stuck them in his coat pocket. "You've heard the expression, 'the eyes are the windows to the soul'?"

Caputo folded the newspaper. "Sure."

Kane continued, "Well, when you look in those windows, you see the devil—Satan himself. No matter what else about the man changes, that never does."

Caputo leaned back in his chair. "Didn't Argari move his entire operation from New York to Pittsburgh?"

"Two years ago. He told everybody that it was easier for him to get around Pittsburgh. He didn't have to commute two hours each way in traffic every day."

Caputo laughed. "Boy! He made it sound like he was driving to a nine-to-five job. The guy was probably chauffeured in from Greenwich—when he *felt* like it.

"Actually, it was Hartsdale. And most of the time people came to him," Kane said. "No, he's here because he didn't have a choice. His cohorts in crime told him a move to Pittsburgh would be better for his health. He's big, but they're bigger. They gave him an opportunity in Pittsburgh he simply couldn't pass up."

"Must've been one hell of an opportunity," Caputo surmised.

"The opportunity of a lifetime. They said, 'Move to Pittsburgh and run the mid-Atlantic region or stay in New York and get sliced and diced, packed in a barrel of lye and dropped to the bottom of the East River.' What would you have done?"

"Wouldn't have taken me long to make the decision." Kane smiled.

"Didn't take him long either. From the time the word hit the street that he was given an ultimatum, to the time he set up shop here—two months. Argari became a Steeler fan real fast."

Caputo signaled the waitress for another coffee. The two men sat quietly for a moment or two. As the waitress was placing the coffee on the table, Kane got up.

"Wait a second, where are you going?" Caputo asked.

Kane tossed a tip onto the table. "I've got a killer to find and I'm not gonna do it talking over coffee."

Caputo turned to the waitress and pointed to the coffee. "Can you put this in a paper cup?"

Kane was out the door and into the lobby before Caputo caught up. "So? Where are you gonna start?"

Kane stopped and turned abruptly to Caputo. "Look, I don't know what your game is, but I work solo. I don't need a partner."

"You don't know the city. I do. I'll take you where ever you want to go—no charge. I wanna help."

Kane thought for a moment. Caputo was right. He didn't know Pittsburgh. Getting around town would be easier with a driver who knew the streets. But was Caputo legit? Whose side was he on?"

"Alright. I've got to go up to my room and get a few things. I'll meet you out front in twenty minutes."

Caputo smiled. "Good. You won't regret it."

"Let's hope *you* don't regret it," Kane said as he turned and walked toward the elevator.

* * * *

"FBI," the man said in an official tone of voice. "Agent Bronson speaking."

Kane was sitting on the edge of his hotel bed. "Maury! Jack Kane. How the hell are you?"

Bronson recognized Kane immediately. "Kane, you old son of a gun! Where are you calling from—some resort in New Hampshire?"

Kane smiled. He thought back to the first time he met Bronson. He was as green as they came—fresh out of the academy. For two years he was Kane's partner, and what had started out as a teacher-student relationship, had grown into a warm personal friendship. Bronson became a good cop. Kane knew that if he stayed with the force, Bronson would rise through the ranks.

The young police officer, however, had other goals. Bronson had wanted to join the FBI. At the end of his second year with the NYPD, he was given the opportunity, and he took advantage of it. Kane had called him at the Bureau's Boston office.

"What's a nice kid from New York doing in a place like Boston? Isn't that the land of the Red Sox, Patriots and Bruins?"

"Hey! I've got a dish in my backyard! I get all the New York stations," Bronson replied. "I probably see more New York games than you do."

Kane always loved Bronson's sense of humor. "That's a definite. I've got rabbit ears on a twelve-year-old portable, and I'm lucky if I can pick up any New York channels."

"So, what can I do for you, partner?" Bronson asked.

Kane put his feet up on the bed and leaned back on the headboard. "I need to find out about somebody."

"One of the bad guys?"

"I'm not sure. He says he's an ex-agent."

"That's easy. Give me his name and I'll call you back in five minutes."

"Thomas Caputo. He says he was booted out of the Bureau in 1989. I think he worked in the Pittsburgh office, but I'm not sure."

"What makes you think Pittsburgh?" asked Bronson.

"Well, that's where I am, right now. It's where I met him."

"Pittsburgh! What the hell are you doing in Pittsburgh?"

Kane rubbed his eyes. He was more tired than he thought. "Just working a case. I'm on my own now, you know."

"I knew you'd never retire and go fishing. C-A-P-U-T-O...Thomas. Give me your number and I'll call you back."

* * * *

The ringing telephone startled Kane. He looked over at the clock on the dresser. Five minutes had become thirty. He must have fallen asleep as soon as he'd hung up the phone.

"Hello?" he sounded as if he'd just awakened.

"I'm double parked out front. You coming down?" It was Caputo.

Kane swung his legs over the edge of the bed and sat up. "Yeah. I'll be right down."

Kane placed the phone on the receiver and stood up. The phone rang again. This time it was Bronson. "Sorry I took so long, old pal. I searched everywhere for a Thomas Caputo."

Kane looked up at the ceiling. "No luck, huh?"

"Well, he's lying about having been an FBI agent."

Kane could tell from Bronson's tone of voice that he had more.

"But you did find something, right?"

"You'd think these guys would be a little smarter—use an alias or something."

"What do you mean?

"I found a Detective Thomas Caputo with the Pittsburgh PD—and he's active."

"He's still on the force?"

"Our computers don't lie." Bronson became serious. "Jack, I don't know what you've got yourself into, but for God's sake, be careful."

"Maury, you're beautiful. I owe you a big New York steak."

"And tickets to the Knicks!" Bronson added.

"You drive a hard bargain, but it's a deal," Kane agreed. "See you soon in New York."

"Stay healthy, partner."

And with that, the conversation was over.

What was Caputo up to? Obviously, their meeting wasn't accidental. Who knew he was coming to Pittsburgh? Who cared? Kaplan's killer, maybe, or perhaps the person who ordered the hit. Kane took his holster from its shipping container and strapped it under his left arm. Then he took out and loaded his .38 and slid that into the holster. Quickly, he put on a light jacket and opened the hotel room door. Caputo was standing on the other side.

"You okay?" There was an untrusting expression on Caputo's face.

"I had to call my ex-wife." It was the first thing that came to mind on such short notice.

"I thought you might be in trouble," Caputo continued.

"Why would I be in trouble? Kane asked. "Nobody knows I'm here."

The two men looked at each other for a moment; each wondering what the other knew. Caputo moved and Kane stepped into the hall. He locked his bedroom door, and the two men started for the elevators.

"Well, where do we begin?"

"I haven't made up my mind yet. I'll tell you in the car."

Of course, Kane had decided. It's just that he didn't want to give Caputo the opportunity to warn Argari that he was on his way.

Chapter Eight

It was a twenty-minute ride from the Hilton to Argari's home in Upper St. Clair—an affluent suburb located ten miles from Pittsburgh, in an area known as the South Hills. Throughout the entire trip, Caputo argued against Kane visiting Argari, but his words fell on deaf ears. Kane would see the gangster with or without him and, although Caputo didn't approve, he wasn't about to let the detective go by himself.

Expensive homes in Upper St. Clair are the norm. Argari's estate, however, made most others look like track houses. It was palatial in every sense of the word. It had a large wrought iron gate, a lawn that equaled the front nine of any exclusive country club, a winding driveway that seemed to go on forever and a house that reflected the elegance and wealth of Tara. But Argari was no Rhett Butler. Caputo stopped the car just across the street from the main gate.

"This is it!" Kane was impressed.

"Yup. The property used to be owned by a president of some steel company," Caputo said. "The guy didn't cut any corners when he built this house."

Kane scanned the wall that followed the perimeter of the land. A rookie could see that it was wired with a complete and sophisticated alarm system.

"There's only one way into that building and that's escorted through the front door, Caputo observed.

"I wouldn't have it any other way."

Kane opened the cab door and stepped out. "You don't have to wait. I don't know how long I'm gonna be. I'm sure I'll be able to get a ride back to the hotel."

"You're nuts! You know that?" Caputo got out of the car and leaned against the back door. "I'll be right here when you get out."

"Just don't leave the meter running." Kane said with a smile.

Kane crossed the street to the gate and looked around. There were two security cameras aimed directly at him. He looked up at the one nearest him and waved.

"Whatever you're selling, we don't want any," said a voice from a small intercom speaker on the right side of the gate.

Kane walked over and leaned close to the unit. "Uh, I'm not selling anything. I'm here to see Mr. Argari."

"Wait a minute," the sentry's voice said tersely.

Kane waited more like five minutes before anything happened. The detective heard the golf cart before he actually saw it come around a bend at the far end of the driveway. He looked back at Caputo and shrugged his shoulders. Both men seemed to notice, at the same time, that the cart was smaller than the driver.

"I hope this guy's just playing golf," Caputo yelled over to Kane.

"I hope he's fat and outta shape!" Kane answered.

When he turned back, the cart was much closer, and Kane could easily see that Toma was anything but fat and out of shape. Argari's assistant steered the cart off the driveway and stopped about ten feet away from the gate. Toma sized up Kane for a moment, and then stepped out and walked the rest of the way to the gate.

"What do you want?"

Toma was an intimidating figure who had a substantial criminal reputation of his own. Once he was up close, Kane knew who he was.

"My name's—"

Toma interrupted, "Jack Kane! We know. Follow me."

Toma punched in the combination to the electronic lock and the gates swung open. As the detective was getting into the cart, he noticed Toma looking across the street toward Caputo. It was a quick look of recognition but it confirmed Kane's suspicions. Toma and Caputo knew each other.

The ride up the driveway to the main house was quicker than Kane thought it would be. Toma jumped out. "This way."

Toma was already through the front door. Kane had to hurry to catch up with him. The interior of the mansion was every bit as magnificent as the exterior. The two men crossed a large vestibule and stopped at the entrance to a small office.

Toma turned and placed his hand on Kane's chest. "Wait here."

Toma turned again and entered the room. Less than a minute later he returned.

"Alright Kane, Mr. Argari will see you. But first—" He pointed to the wall. "You know the routine."

Kane put his arms against the wall and spread his legs.

"I'll save you some time. My gun's in my shoulder holster."

Toma took the weapon and held it in front of Kane's face. "You got a permit for this thing?" He smiled when he asked the question.

"Yeah, I've got a permit."

"I'm sure you've got one in New York, but what about Pennsylvania?"

Kane nodded his head. "It's taken care of. Don't worry about it."

"I hope so. I'd hate to see you get in trouble." He really didn't care. "Now, what else you hiding?"

The frisking was unusually rough. Toma enjoyed manhandling the ex-cop.

"You had enough fun?" Kane asked.

Toma stuck the gun in his belt. "You can pick this up on the way out."

Kane pointed toward the weapon. "Be careful. It's got a hair trigger. I wouldn't want you to shoot your nuts off."

Toma motioned for Kane to move. "At least I've got balls, Kane."

* * * *

Argari was standing behind his desk with his back to Kane. He didn't turn to greet him. "You've got balls, Kane."

The detective laughed. "Funny, your sidekick and I were just talking about that!"

Suddenly, Kane felt a sharp punch to the kidney and he buckled to the floor. He looked up to see Toma standing over him. "I thought this would a private conversation, Argari."

Argari was still looking out the window, behind his desk. He showed no surprise. It was as if Argari knew Toma was going to slug Kane. He probably did.

"This *is* a private conversation. Mr. Toma is privy to all that I do."

"Sorta like a vice president. He's ready to take over if anything happens," Kane said as he stood up, this time positioning himself in such a way so that he could see both Toma and Argari at the same time.

The room was silent for a moment, and then Argari slowly turned toward Kane. His expression was fixed and stern. Kane was quick to see the hatred in his eyes.

"Oh, something is going to happen to *one* of us in this room, Kane, but I can assure you it's not going to be Mr. Toma or myself."

"You don't have to hit me in the head with a brick twice for me to get the picture." Kane was rubbing the spot where he'd been hit.

"Oh, but I'd like to," Argari responded quickly. "I didn't invite you to my home, Kane. You would never be welcomed in my house."

"Believe me, Argari, under normal circumstances, I wouldn't come, even if I were invited."

Argari reached for a cigarette. "So, what abnormal circumstances have forced you to pay me this unwelcomed visit?" He stuck the cigarette between his lips and lit it. "This has gotta be good."

"A mutual acquaintance of ours was killed in this adopted hometown of yours, a few days back."

Argari looked puzzled. "Would I have read about this in the paper?"

Kane was so angry now, he had completely forgotten about the pain in his back. He had always wanted to put Argari behind bars, but the criminal was like the proverbial fish—the one that always got away. He was finding it hard to maintain his composure, but he did it.

"Hell, you would have seen it on TV, too. Sheldon Kaplan—a guy from the old neighborhood. Some no good son of a bitch—some lowlife—had him hit! Can you believe that?"

A look of satisfaction appeared on Argari's face, and he smiled.

"Sheldon Kaplan! If I remember correctly, he was one of your prize informants, Kane. He was the punk who set up my brother. The guy who gave you the opportunity to ice my flesh and blood. He was dead a long time ago. He died the day you killed my brother. He just didn't know it yet." Argari blew some smoke in Kane's direction.

"So you admit killing him?" Kane continued.

Argari shrugged his shoulders and rolled his eyes in mock innocence. "What are you talking about, Kane? I didn't hear me say nothing about killing nobody! Did you Toma?"

"Sounds to me like this guy's hallucinating or something, Boss," Toma answered.

Kane reached into his coat pocket, but Toma was quick to grab his wrist.

"Relax. It's just some pictures," Kane said showing him the corner of the envelope.

Argari waved him off. "It's okay, Alonzo. Let's see his pictures."

Kane took them out and placed them on Argari's desk, one by one.

"You like these?"

Argari leaned over and examined them. "The lighting could be better."

Toma laughed. Kane glanced over at him and then back to Argari. "You'll never guess where I found these."

"Let me guess. You bought 'em at a gift shop at the airport."

Toma laughed again.

Kane continued, "I found them in a file at Sheldon Kaplan's office. My guess is, he had something on you and you found out about it, suckered him into coming out here—probably told him you had some work for him—and then popped him."

`Kane tapped the pictures. "And this is what he had on you."

Now Argari laughed. "What? I supposedly had him hit because he found out I'm a baseball fan? Since when is it a crime to talk to a pitcher?"

"Maybe you were bribing him. Maybe you were fixing a game. Maybe he's one of your men. All I know is that whatever it was, it wasn't kosher."

"Prove it," Argari challenged.

Kane smiled. "That's exactly what I'm gonna do."

The detective turned and walked over to Toma. "I'll take my gun now. I'm leaving."

Toma looked over at Argari for his approval. He nodded that it was alright. He pulled the gun from his belt, opened the cylinder and dropped all of the ammunition on to the floor.

"You can have the gun back, but the bullets stay here."

Kane took the weapon. "I can get more."

As Kane walked toward the door, Argari yelled to him. "You're not a cop anymore, Kane. You don't have any jurisdiction here."

Kane stopped and turned back to the mobster. "This isn't professional, Argari. This is personal."

He turned away and walked out of the room. Argari motioned to Toma. "Escort him to the gate. We don't want him snooping around."

Toma caught up with Kane and took him by the arm. Kane stopped abruptly. "Let go of my arm."

Toma tightened his grip. "Not until you're off the property."

Kane slammed his free hand into Toma's crotch and squeezed. Toma released him quickly but Kane continued the hold. It hurt so much, Toma could only open his mouth. He was too paralyzed to scream.

"Listen. Next time you put your hand on me, you'd better kill me—or I'll kill you. You got it?"

Toma couldn't respond. Kane squeezed a bit harder.

"You got it?" he yelled louder.

"We've all got it," Argari yelled from the office doorway. "Now, unless you're getting some weirdo kick outta that, I suggest you let him go."

Kane looked at Argari for a moment, then back to Toma. "You were right Toma. You *do* have balls."

He let go of Toma's testicles, and the hood slumped to the floor and curled up in a fetal position with both hands between his legs.

Kane walked to the door. "See ya real soon, Argari."

Argari flipped him the middle finger. "Sooner than you think, you mother—"

The door slammed behind Kane and censored Argari's final remark. But Kane got the gist of it.

Chapter Nine

Reece stared in at the signal, brought the ball and glove to his belt, looked at first, paused at second and then delivered the pitch. The fast ball popped into the catcher's mitt.

"Nice. Real nice," yelled the pitching coach. "Give me a couple more like that and you can call it a day."

"No problem! It feels good," Reece responded.

The coach took a small package of sunflower seeds from his jacket pocket and tossed a few into his mouth.

"Boy, that kid's got a helluva fast ball."

The instructor turned and looked at the stranger standing on the other side of the fence. "Best in the major leagues," he replied. "You with the press?"

Kane shook his head. "No. Actually, I'm just a retired New York City cop who loves baseball, and when I'm not at the games, I sneak into ballparks and watch the teams practice. Sometimes you guys throw me out, sometimes you let me stay."

The coach smiled as he took off his hat. "New York, huh? I'm an old New York City boy myself—born and raised in Queens."

Kane knew who he was as soon as he saw the red hair. "Red' Linderman! I saw you pitch for the Yankees in the '77 World Series."

"Yeah. We lost the series."

"I know, but you won that game."

Linderman smiled. "Well, that wasn't one of my better outings. I was getting shelled, but fortunately for me, Tommy Lapolata was getting shelled even worst by our guys.

"The Yankees were quite a team back in those days."

"This is a pretty good team, too!"

"I guess so! National League East Champions two years in a row. If you can hold them together, you've got some great years of baseball ahead of you."

Linderman walked back to the fence and leaned against it. "The dam's gotta burst someday. These salaries are gonna kill the game. Pretty soon the fellas on the bench are going to be demanding a million plus. The game's gonna go outta business. Hopefully I'll be retired by then."

"Red, can I talk to you for a minute?" the manager yelled from across the field.

"Gotta go. Good talking to you." Linderman said as he started to walk away. He turned to Reece. "Johnny, you can call it a day, whenever you want."

Kane watched Reece throw a few more pitches—each one with the same blistering speed and accuracy. When he was finished, Reece picked up a towel, that was lying next to the mound, wiped the sweat from his face and arms, threw it over his shoulder and started for the dugout. Kane had walked as close as he could to the side Reece was entering.

"Johnny! Johnny Reece! Can I talk to you for a second?"

Reece looked over and waved him off. "Sorry, gotta take a shower."

Kane persisted. "You really should look at this picture."

Reece stopped and took a deep breath. "I don't do autographs. I never have. I would think a guy your age would have better things to do."

Kane leaned over the railing and held the picture up to Reece. "I don't want your damned autograph! All I want you to do is look at this picture."

"Listen, pal—"

Kane interrupted, "I'm not your pal. This picture has nothing to do with baseball."

Reece hesitated but his curiosity got the best of him. The ballplayer stepped closer and examined the image. His mouth dropped open a bit.

"Where did you get this?" he asked as he grabbed it from Kane's hand.

Kane smiled. "By all means, keep it. As a matter of fact, here's the rest of the set," he said, as he tossed an envelope at him. "I mean, why shouldn't you have them. After all, I gave Argari a set."

Reece look up at Kane. "This guy's just a fan."

Kane became deadly serious. "'Fan, my ass! You and Argari are connected. He likes baseball as much as I like heavy metal."

Reece put the pictures back into the envelope and stuck it in his pants pocket. He threw his glove onto the bench and then sat down. "People take pictures of me every day. It goes with the territory."

"This guy's one of the country's most notorious gangsters."

"Yeah, well I had my picture taken with the Bishop last week. What's that mean—I'm gonna be a priest?"

"No. I don't think you're the priestly type."

Kane was starting to get to Reece. "Hey, I asked you before—where'd you get these pictures?"

Kane was looking out at the playing field. "I got them from a friend of mine."

He looked back at Reece. "I think you met him, too. His name was Shelley Kaplan."

Reece was good. The only hint of recognition was a slight but sudden movement in his eyes.

"What makes you think I know anyone named Kaplan?"

"No, that's *knew* him—past tense. You see, he was the recipient of the ultimate 'beaning.'"

"Ultimate beaning? What the hell are you talking about?"

"Someone threw at his head. Only he didn't throw a baseball, he threw a bullet. And he didn't brush Kaplan back, he killed him."

Reece picked up his glove and stood up. "Who are you and what's all this got to do with me?"

"Name's Kane—Jack Kane. I'm a private investigator from New York. I came to Pittsburgh to find Kaplan's murderer."

"And you think I had something to do with it," Reece concluded.

"I think there's a strong possibility," Kane answered.

Reece seemed to be insulted. "I've never had anyone call me a murderer!"

"There's a first time for everything," Kane said. "You see, Kaplan wrote something on the back of one of the pictures—one of the originals that I have locked away."

"What kinda something?" Reece asked sarcastically.

Kane reached into his coat pocket and took out a small note pad. He flipped a few pages until he found what he wanted.

"Well, if this means what I think it means, this something's incriminating. You see, Kaplan wrote: "May 9th—Santori Shooting—GCT platform" on the back of one of your pictures."

"So?"

"The Pirates were playing the Mets on May 9th—an afternoon game. Santori was shot about 10:30 that night. He was killed the same way Shelley was killed." Kane tapped the back of his neck. "One strategically placed slug, fired at an upward angle from close range into the base of his skull."

"You think it's me! Why the hell would I do something like that?"

Kane shook his head slowly. "Damned if I know! You've got the world by the tail. Santori was underworld. He was a rogue bull. He didn't have a lot of friends in the industry. He kept sticking his nose into everyone else's business. There was a rumor on the street that he was going to be taken out, but when nothing happened after a few weeks, everyone kinda forgot about it. What might have happened was you were waiting for the Mets series to come up in the schedule. It's the perfect cover—a major league ballplayer who is actually a hired assassin. You fly in with the club. No one checks you out. You commit your hit, play your game and escape with the team."

For a moment, Kane thought he saw a touch of madness in Reece's eyes. Then Reece seemed to turn cold and deliberate. "You're talking through your hat. This is all circumstantial evidence. You can't prove a damned thing."

"Well, for the time being, you're right. But I've got a feeling that when I look back at your schedule for the past few years, I'll be able to find similar unsolved shootings in the towns where you played, on the dates your team was in those towns."

Reece smiled. "Boy, you're reaching a little, aren't you Kane? I made over two million dollars throwing a baseball last year. Why would I risk all of that?"

"Maybe for the thrills Maybe for the money. Maybe because you're nuts."

Reece laughed. "You're not the first person who thought I might be a little nuts."

The ballplayer stepped into the hallway that ran from the dugout to the clubhouse, and stopped. "Mr. Kane, this is a lot of bull if you ask me. I've got better things to do with my spare time than hunt people down and kill them."

"Have you?" Kane asked.

There was silence for a moment and then Reece stepped back into the dugout. There was a menacing look on his face. He looked right into the detective's eyes. "Aren't you taking a helluva gamble Kane?"

"What do mean?"

"Well, if what you say is true and I am the killer you're looking for, don't you think there's a better than average chance that I'm gonna have to take you out now? If I am that guy, after what you just told me, you've left me no choice."

There was a certain challenging tone in Reece's voice. Kane knew the pieces were coming together.

"You're overlooking one important point, Mr. Reece."

"What's that?"

"You see, if my supposition is correct and you are the murderer, I have a very significant advantage over your other victims. I know what you are and I know what you look like. I'll be ready."

Kane turned and walked up the aisle toward the exit. Reece leaned over the dugout railing, made an invisible gun with his hand and fired. "Bang! You're dead," he said softly to himself.

Although he didn't turn back, Kane knew Reece was watching him. He stepped into the concession area, and Caputo appeared from behind a support.

"You believe in taking chances, don't you?"

"You're everywhere, aren't you Caputo?" Kane sounded annoyed.

The two men started to walk together.

"I'm just trying to help. You may need someone to cover your backside."

"I've covered my backside by myself for a lot of years now, and done a pretty good job" Kane said.

Kane was moving at a fast pace, and Caputo had to hurry to keep up with him.

"Let's see if I've got this straight," Caputo continued. "In a matter of just a few hours you've managed to piss off one of the underworld's most ruthless characters and possibly one of the deadliest assassins of our time. I'd say you're on a roll."

"I pissed off Argari a long time ago, when I shot his brother. As for Reece—I never liked his pitching style anyway."

Caputo pulled at his shirt collar. "Boy, I think it's getting hot in here."

"It won't boil unless you turn up the heat," Kane answered.

Chapter Ten

Kane sat in his hotel bedroom jotting down notes on all that had taken place since he arrived in Pittsburgh and trying to make sense of it. Anyone who knows Pittsburgh will attest to the fact that its weather changes as quickly as women's dress styles. What had been a beautiful day, dissolved into a stormy night full of wind, rain, thunder and lightning. Kane had asked for this room because it overlooked Pittsburgh's landmark Point State Park. Any hope of enjoying the view was dashed by the heavy and constant stream of rain that fell against his window.

He was just starting to doze off when his phone rang. It startled him. He instinctively grabbed his pistol, which he had placed on the side table next to him, and jumped to his feet. It took only a moment for him to realize where the noise was coming from.

"You're getting old," he said to himself. "You were never this jumpy when you were on the force."

He tossed the gun on to the bed and answered the telephone.

"Mr. Kane?"

"Yes," he replied.

"This is the front desk calling. You had left instructions for us to call you if anyone asked for your room number."

"That's right."

"Well, your guest is on his way up."

"You mean Mr. Caputo, the cab driver you've seen me with?"

"No, no. We know Mr. Caputo. This is someone else."

Just then, Kane heard the door handle jiggle.

"If there's anything we ca—"

Kane placed the receiver on the phone and terminated the conversation. He immediately flicked off the light switch next to his bed and pulled off his shoes so that his movement would be quieter. Carefully, he walked to the door and looked out through the eyepiece. The hall was dark but lit well enough for him to see that he didn't recognize the intruder. The man seemed big and powerful. Kane knew that he wasn't here to make small talk.

Kane figured he'd have a few minutes before the unwelcome guest could pick the lock on the door. What he hadn't counted on was the man having a master key. Kane heard the lock release. He slid the flimsy chain lock across the door.

"This should hold him for about ten seconds."

Kane felt his way in the darkness back to where he'd been sitting. The door popped open but the chain held momentarily. Kane reached for his pistol but realized, as soon as his hand touched the empty table top, that he had thrown it onto the bed when he answered the phone.

"Son of a bitch!" he whispered.

He heard metal against metal and knew the intruder had come well equipped. He was using a small metal cutter to snap the chain. Kane hurried into the bathroom and hid in the darkness. There wasn't much else he could do with so little time.

The chain broke and Kane held his breath. The man stepped into the dark room—his shape silhouetted by the hall light. He was so close Kane could smell his aftershave. Confidently, the assassin raised his silencer-equipped pistol and fired into the empty bed. It couldn't have taken any longer then a few seconds but to Kane it felt like an eternity. He could hear each cough of the gun followed by a thud from the bullet impacting the mattress. He fired four rounds. This killer wasn't taking any chances.

Kane knew the man would turn on the lights in order to verify his work. He'd immediately see what he'd done, find Kane and finish the job. Kane's only chance for survival was to surprise the killer in the dark. There was no time to rethink his options. He had to move, and he had to move now.

Kane grabbed the man's arm that was holding the gun and pulled it down hard across his knee. The man screamed but didn't drop the pistol. It was Kane's first indication of his opponent's strength. The second indication was the sharp and painful punch he felt in his ribs. Kane wanted to grab his side but he knew that if he let go of the arm the man would most certainly shoot him. He held on for dear life.

The two men struggled and tumbled around the room. A lamp was broken, a table smashed and a chair was knocked aside. During the commotion, the gun discharged. The bullet punctured and weakened the picture window but didn't shatter it. The two men fell to the floor, and before the detective could do anything about it, the killer was on top. They fought desperately for control of the weapon. Several times the barrel waved in front of Kane's face, but not long enough for the attacker to squeeze off a round.

The assailant must have had a good thirty-five pounds on Kane and he used every ounce to his advantage. The fight was beginning to exhaust Kane. If he was to win, he had to finish it soon. Suddenly, the killer switched from trying to pull the gun away to pushing his forearm into Kane's face. It was desperation time. Kane bit hard into his opponent's arm—so hard he could feel the muscle tear. The man screamed, dropped the pistol and pulled back, shifting his weight. Kane pushed with both hands and the attacker tumbled backward. Kane tried to stand, slipped on some bed covers and fell onto the bed. He looked up, saw the big man stand and then lunge toward him. Kane stopped his forward progress with both feet and, with all the energy he could muster, pushed him away.

The weakened window pane shattered into a thousand small pieces as the intruder's body crashed through. It happened so quickly, Kane wasn't sure if the man had had time to scream. He took a moment to rest and catch his breath. All that Kane could hear now were the sounds of the city and the wild weather swirling by the open window.

* * * *

It had been a trying night. The police interrogation proved to be long and repetitious. Kane was physically and emotionally exhausted. The hotel had moved him to another room just down the hall, but getting sleep at this point was impossible. The police were constantly coming down to the room and asking "one more very important question." And it didn't surprise Kane when Caputo showed up carrying two cups of Dunkin Donut's coffee.

"You look like hell!" Caputo was standing in the doorway.

Kane was sitting in a chair next to the window. He didn't bother to look up. He recognized the voice.

"You know, Caputo, you're like lint on a new suit. You can brush it till hell freezes over but more lint keeps popping up."

Caputo walked in and placed the coffee on the dresser.

"You know, Kane, I've been compared to a lot of things—but lint! That's a new one."

Caputo took the cups out, rolled up the bag and tossed it into a wastebasket on the other side of the room. Kane looked up.

"So I guess now you're gonna tell me you just happened to be dropping off a fare' when our friend did a double somersault out my window."

Caputo handed a coffee to Kane. "I hope it's the way you like it."

Kane was too tired to care how the coffee was prepared.

"Look Jack, I'm not gonna play any more games," Caputo continued. "Someone's just tried to kill you, and that changes everything."

Kane sipped his coffee and listened.

"This ain't easy, but remember the story about me being with the FBI?"

Kane didn't answer.

"Well—I'm not with the FBI. I've never been with the FBI. I'm—"

"A cop," Kane said calmly.

Caputo thought for a moment, smiled and then sat on the edge of the bed facing Kane. "You've known all along, haven't you?"

Kane swallowed another mouthful of coffee. He wasn't a big coffee drinker but this tasted surprisingly good.

"You know, Caputo, I look like a country bumpkin, I kinda act like a country bumpkin, but I was on the force doing the same thing you're doing for a long, long time. I called my friends in the Bureau and checked you out as soon as I had a free moment. Besides, you're the worst cab driver I've ever driven with."

"I am?"

"You're too polite. You've gotta be a little crazy to drive a cab—even in Pittsburgh."

Caputo put his coffee cup down on the night table. Suddenly, he wasn't thirsty anymore.

"What else do you know?" he asked.

"I know that as soon as I arrived, you were on me like a wet blanket. If I sneezed you'd say, 'Excuse me.'"

Caputo smiled. "And I thought I was good at this undercover stuff."

"What I don't know is how you knew I was coming," Kane continued.

Caputo hesitated, as if deciding whether or not Kane could be trusted. He said, "Lauder told me word on the street was that you were directly involved in the Kaplan murder. His informants told him that you were on your way here."

"Word on the street, my ass! Hell, I didn't know I was coming to Pittsburgh until a few hours before I got on the plane."

The two men sat quietly for a moment, considering the possibilities.

"No, I've known him too long. It can't be him." Caputo was thinking out loud.

"Lauder! At this point, everything kinda points in his direction," Kane surmised.

"I'm gonna have to think on that one, Jack. He's been too good a cop for too many years to get mixed up in stuff like this," Caputo said as he sighed.

It was obvious to Kane that the idea troubled the younger detective. "Caputo, I've seen it happen to the best of them. They do it for the craziest reasons. I knew a guy who had twenty-nine years on the force—I mean, he had an impeccable record. He blew it because of a bad gambling debt. Pension, reputation—everything right out the window."

Caputo looked at Kane but said nothing.

"What do you know about the guy who tried to take me out?" Kane asked, changing the subject.

Caputo rubbed his eyes. "His name's Charles Meanny."

"An appropriate name."

"He's one of the best in the business."

Kane corrected Caputo. "*Was* one of the best in the business."

Caputo smiled. "I stand corrected. Up until an hour ago, he *was* one of the best in the business. He was also one of Alonzo Toma's lovers."

Kane's eyes widened. "Whoa! Wait a second! You mean Toma's—gay?"

"Yup."

"Does Argari know about this?"

"Sure. He uses it to keep Toma in line. He threatens to hurt one of Toma's boyfriends or maybe tell his traditional Italian Catholic family their son's a homosexual, if he doesn't tow the line."

"It's a new world. Homosexuality's not as big a deal as it was years ago."

"To a traditional Italian Catholic family it's a big deal."

Kane thought for a moment. "You think this was Argari's doing?"

"Argari hated Meanny. He wouldn't allow him on the property."

"So you think this came from Toma," Kane concluded.

"Probably." Caputo smiled. "I don't know what you did when you paid Mr. Argari that little visit, but whatever it was, you really must've pissed off Toma."

Kane visualized Toma grabbing his nuts and rolling around in pain on Argari's floor. "Yeah, I guess you could say that."

"Look, Kane, why don't you get some sleep. I'm gonna post a guard."

"You don't need to do that!" Kane protested.

"It's just for the night. Tomorrow morning, I'll pick you up and we can try to make some sense outta all this."

Kane was exhausted. Sleep sounded real good to him right then.

"What are you gonna do?" Kane asked.

Caputo got up and walked to the door. "I've got a few things to do downtown and then I'm gonna call it a night, too. I'll pick you up about nine. Good night Jack," Caputo said as he closed the door.

Kane got up, took a couple of steps and collapsed onto the bed. He planned on resting his eyes for a moment, but he was asleep in a matter of seconds.

Chapter Eleven

Lauder opened his eyes. A noise—he'd heard a noise! But where'd it come from? What time was it? It took a second for his eyes to bring into focus the clock on the night table. 3:10 a.m..

"What? That can't be right," he thought.

Then he heard it again. It wasn't a loud banging, more like a polite knock. But who'd be politely knocking on his front door at 3:10 a.m.? Lauder sat up, wiped his eyes and looked around the room for his bathrobe. He stood, walked over to a chair, grabbed the robe and put it on. There was the knocking again.

He moistened his lips and thought, "My gun. I'd better take my gun."

Lauder walked to the closet. He pulled open the door and found the holster he had left hanging on a coat hook. He took out the revolver and popped the cylinder to make certain it was loaded. When he was younger and had a family, he never left a loaded gun around the house. Now his children were grown and his wife was dead. All the reasons were gone. Every chamber was full.

Except for the small night light in his room, the house was dark. Lauder's bedroom was on the second floor. He was about to turn on the light switch at the top of the stairs but he stopped himself. Whatever little advantage he might have would most certainly be lost by turning on the lights. He was halfway down the stairs when the visitor knocked again. It was louder this time, but then he was closer to the door.

It was a solid entrance with only two small translucent glass panes at the top of the door. Lauder spied the stranger through the eyepiece in the door, but because the light on the porch was off, all he could see was the silhouette of a man, backlit by the street light in front of the house. Lauder slipped the pistol into his robe pocket.

"Who's there?" he yelled.

"It's me! Open up," came the response.

It was a familiar voice, but he still wasn't sure who 'me' was. He flipped on the outside light and looked through the eyepiece again.

"Oh, it's you," he said.

He threw the bolt back and pulled open the door. "What the hell are you doing coming by at this hour of the morning?"

"I have to talk. Something's come up."

"Does Argari know you're here?"

"Of course he doesn't. You gonna invite me in or what?"

Toma had on a light coat; it was an unseasonably cool night, but he was shivering for another reason. Lauder stepped aside.

"Yeah, come on in."

Toma gestured to the bulge in Lauder's bathrobe as he entered the house. "You can put that foolish gun away."

"You don't miss a trick, do you?"

He turned to Toma. "I'll be the one who decides if I need it or not. Now, what's going on?"

Toma turned, walked into the living room and sat down. "You got something to drink?"

"You want something to drink, go to an all-night diner," Lauder said.

Toma smiled and sat back in the chair. "You haven't much use for me have you?"

"Look, if you got me outta bed to discuss our relationship, I'm afraid I'm gonna have to ask you to leave."

Toma raised his hand. "Alright, no more bullshit. I'll get right to the point. You know that nosy cop, Kane?"

Lauder came closer, his hand still on the pistol grip. "Yeah, what about him?"

"I tried to have him taken out tonight."

Lauder's eyes widened and his face filled with rage. "You tried to hit a cop?"

"He's not a cop anymore. He's a PI."

"Once a cop, always a cop," Lauder said, shaking his head in disbelief. "Boy, I've gotta hand it to you, you've got a lotta balls coming by my house and telling me this. What makes you think I won't take you in myself?"

Toma leaned forward in the chair again. "I can think of two reasons. The first is, if they found out you were working for Argari, they'd lock you up and throw away the key. It goes without saying what would happen to you in prison. But the second reason is the one I'd worry about if I were you."

"And what's that?"

"Number two is—I'd slit your throat from ear to ear." Toma pulled a long stiletto knife from inside his coat sleeve. "You wouldn't want me to do that now, would you?"

"Aren't you forgetting one thing? I have a gun." Lauder pulled the pistol from the robe.

"You'd be dead before you could pull the trigger," Toma said, matter-of-factly. "But enough of this. We've other, more important things to talk about." Toma folded the blade and put the knife away.

Lauder lowered the gun, but still held onto it. "You said *tried?* I take it you blew it."

"I'm not sure I like the way you phrased that. I lost a good friend tonight."

"Who?"

"Chuck Meanny."

"That faggy creep! The world's a better place without him," Lauder said.

Toma took offense. "Listen, you keep flapping your trap like that and life's gonna get a whole lot harder for you."

"You didn't come by to make funeral arrangements. Get to the point."

"The cop threw Chuckie out his damned hotel room window. The poor guy did a swan dive right into a parked car."

"How many floors?"

"I don't know—seven, eight, maybe ten. I couldn't be sure from where I was parked. All I heard was glass breaking and then this loud thud. I don't even think the poor guy had time to scream. I was gonna get out and see what happened, but the next thing I knew, the place was crawling with cops. They were everywhere."

"You were waiting for him?"

"Yeah. I drove him over."

"Argari didn't order this hit? You did, right?" Lauder asked.

"Argari's getting old. His days are numbered. One second he's thinking rationally and the next second he's talking crazy."

"What do you mean?"

"I didn't mind so much him wanting to kill Kane. After what happened to his brother, that seemed fair to me. But first he wanted it done quickly, and then he wanted to tie it into this weekend's job. He's gonna screw it all up. If the big guys find out, they'll get rid of every one of us."

It was clearer to Lauder now. "Oh, so you figured if you bump off Kane, Argari can't screw up the big hit."

"Problem is, Kane's still alive and I think he knows that Caputo's a cop."

"What make's you say that?"

"Caputo showed up. He walked into the hotel like a cab driver, but when he came out, he was flashing his badge to people and walking around the crime scene. He wasn't hiding the fact that he's a cop. That tells me that he told Kane. He wasn't playacting anymore."

"Maybe Kane was asleep," Lauder said.

"Hey! I'm not a genius, but I know that a good undercover cop never steps outta character until the game's over. The little masquerade game with Kane—believe me, it's over."

Suddenly, the room had become uncomfortably warm. Lauder walked to the window and looked out. "If what you're saying is true, I could be in a lot of deep shit. Caputo's smart. He'll put two and two together and be onto me before you know it."

"That's why I'm here. Take him off the case. Put him somewhere else—anywhere else, but get him away from Kane."

"What about Argari? When he finds out what happened tonight, he'll have your ass."

"Let me worry about Argari. Just take care of Caputo."

Lauder wiped some perspiration from his forehead and then opened the window.

"What's the matter, Lauder? You look a scared."

"I am scared. This whole thing's coming apart. Transferring Caputo's not gonna stop him. Hell, if he's suspicious, it'll just confirm his suspicions."

Toma looked down at the floor, thought for a moment and then turned back to Lauder. "You're right. Caputo's probably onto us already. You'll just have to kill the son of a bitch."

Lauder was a terrific inside person—an important conduit of information from the department to Argari's ears, but he wasn't a gunman. True, he'd iced a few people in the name of self-preservation, but he never got used to it. It wasn't something he could just forget.

"Aw, dammit Toma, I can't just pop the kid! What the hell do you think I'm made of?"

Toma got up. "I don't care what you're made of. Caputo's your responsibility. It was your idea to use him, now you're gonna have to dispose of him. He can mess it up for—"

Branches snapped in the bushes just outside the window.

"Wait!" Lauder waved his arm to silence Toma. "Did you hear that?"

"Probably a cat or something."

"Did anyone follow you here?" Lauder asked.

"Hell no. You think I'm stupid?" Toma answered.

Lauder leaned over and looked intently into the night. "I don't like it." He raised the pistol. "I think someone's out there."

He turned back. Toma was already at the door, Beretta in hand. Lauder followed him onto the porch.

The two men spoke in whispers. "You go around that way." Toma pointed. "I'll go the opposite way. If there's anyone out here, we'll find out soon enough."

* * * *

The small yard was bathed in darkness. It was a starless, moonless night and that just made the darkness darker. Lauder gripped the gun tightly. His eyes strained to catch a glimpse of something—anything. He walked slowly and cautiously around the corner of his house. There were larger, unmanicured bushes framing the building's perimeter. It would be easy for an intruder to hide behind them. As he walked, he noticed a pumping sound. He hesitated. It was his heart. He put his hand to his chest. It felt as if it were going to explode. He took a deep breath and then another step. Suddenly, he felt the tip of a gun barrel against his temple. Lauder was sure he felt his heart stop.

"You miserable bastard." Caputo stepped from behind a large shrub. "I didn't believe it. Kane suspected you but I thought he was full of it. I respected you like a father!"

Caputo pulled the hammer back in anger, as if to fire. "I oughta blow your brains out, right here."

Lauder lowered his eyes. "If it'll make you feel better."

Caputo hesitated a moment and then uncocked the gun. "Where's that sick pervert, Toma?"

There was a tap on his shoulder. "Yoo-hoo! Here I am!"

As Caputo was spinning around, Toma's gun butt caught him on the side of the face and he collapsed, unconscious.

"Well, I'll be damned! You were right. Someone was out here. And how convenient—the very man we've got to get rid of."

"We've got to get rid of?" Lauder asked.

"Seeing that he's here, I may as well help you," Toma said with a smile. "Besides, I don't like being called a sick pervert."

"You're not gonna do it here? The neighbors will hear."

"Of course not. We'll put him in the trunk and drive him out to the woods."

"I can't do it," Lauder said. "I'm too close to the kid."

Toma put his hand on Lauder's shoulder. "Don't worry. You do the driving; I'll do the killing. Now let's get a move on."

Toma grabbed Caputo under the armpits and Lauder took his feet.

"We'll use my car. It's parked in front of the garage," Lauder said. "This way we don't have to carry him into the street."

Caputo wasn't a large man, but he wasn't small either. Both men had to exert some energy, carrying his one-hundred-and-eighty pounds to the car.

"Damn! My keys are in the house."

Toma wasn't happy. "Well, get them!"

They placed Caputo on the driveway and Lauder disappeared into the darkness. Caputo moaned and Toma looked down at him.

"Oh please don't wake up. I really don't want to have to kill you here."

Caputo was just conscious enough to hear and comprehend the threat. The more lucid he became, the more he felt the pain from the welt on his face. A moment or two later, he heard footsteps and he knew Lauder had returned.

"I got the keys!" he said.

"I'm proud of you." Toma answered sarcastically.

Caputo heard the keys jangle and then the trunk pop open. Next, he felt the two men lift and drop him into the trunk. He knew that his best chance was to continue to pretend to be unconscious. A minute or two later, the car doors opened and closed, the engine started and the vehicle began to move—backward at first and then quickly forward. It was a clean trunk, as trunks go, and Caputo was amazed at how clearly he could hear both Lauder and Toma. Then he noticed the smell of fumes.

"Oh no! Lauder must have a hole in his exhaust," he thought. If he didn't get out of that trunk fast, he'd die from carbon monoxide poisoning. There was no light whatsoever in the trunk, so he had to feel around in the darkness for something that might help him break the lock. Then, without warning, he coughed.

"Damn!" Caputo thought.

"What was that?" he heard Toma ask.

"I don't know!" Lauder answered.

"Let's check him."

Caputo felt the car slow to a stop. The door opened and someone walked to the back. Maybe it was an act of God or simply dumb luck, but for no special reason he moved his left hand and felt the L-shaped tire iron. The trunk light was burned out and it had been too dark for Toma or Lauder to see the tool lying on the floor. Then he heard the keys rattle and the lock release. There was no time to think this plan through. It was do it or die! Whoever was doing the checking seemed to take forever opening the trunk. When Caputo saw the bathrobe, he knew who it was immediately. His grip tightened on the tire iron.

"For God's sake, will you hurry?" Toma yelled.

"Shut up! You got me into this," Lauder responded.

And then the trunk was open. Because of the darkness, Lauder leaned in to get a better look. Caputo swung the iron and caught the man behind the right ear. Lauder groaned and slumped to the ground. Caputo didn't waste any time. As he was climbing out of the trunk, Toma felt the back of the car rise and he knew his prisoner was escaping. He grabbed the door handle with his right hand and his gun with his left.

"No you don't, you son of a bitch!" Toma yelled.

But by the time he was out of the car, Caputo had disappeared into the woods. Toma walked to the back just as Lauder was getting to his feet.

"What happened?" Toma screamed.

"How the hell do I know!" Lauder yelled back. He was holding the side of his head and he knew the warm liquid running down his arm was his blood. Toma took out a cigarette lighter and flicked it on. Lauder was covered with blood.

"Looks like he hit you with a baseball bat." Then he noticed the tire iron laying at his feet. "Or maybe a tire iron." Toma reached down and retrieved it. "You shouldn't leave these things lying around, Lauder."

"Listen Toma, this arrangement's falling apart." There was panic in Lauder's voice. "Argari and I agreed—all you guys wanted from me was information and inside help, that's it. What you do is your business. I never said I'd get involved with any of your dirty work. Now Caputo's gonna go back, tell them what happened tonight and everything's gonna turn to shit! I've gotta talk to them—explain the situation. Maybe they'll cut me a break."

It was obvious to Toma that Lauder was going into shock. He was starting to ramble and sound desperate. Toma knew that Lauder needed to see a doctor right away. He also knew that if Lauder saw a doctor, he'd repeat his story. He couldn't risk it. He had no other option.

"Hey, is that Caputo?" Toma pointed down the road.

Lauder turned. The gangster raised his arm high and with all of his energy, slammed the tire iron across the top of the man's skull. It split open like a fresh watermelon. Lauder was dead instantly.

"Sorry. This wasn't my plan, but sometimes you gotta do the unexpected," Toma said to the corpse.

He pulled off Lauder's bathrobe and wrapped it around his head to keep the brains and blood from getting all over the trunk. It took him a couple of minutes to load the body into the car. Then he turned toward the woods.

"I know you can hear me, Caputo. You better die in those woods because as soon as you show your face, you're dead."

He stood silently for a moment, listening for a sound that might give away Caputo's location. All he heard was an owl. Then he walked back to the car, got in and drove off.

Caputo watched the tail lights disappear down the road. There had been enough light for him to see most of it. And he was close enough to hear the blow and the sound of Lauder's body hitting the pavement. He knew what had happened. A man who had made some bad choices at the end of his career, had just paid for those choices. It started to rain, but he didn't move from behind the rocks for at least an hour.

Chapter Twelve

Reece opened his eyes and saw Toma staring down at him. He tried to sit up, but Toma put his hand on his shoulder.

"Relax!" he said in a calm voice.

Reece ran a hand through his messy hair. "How the hell did you get in here, anyway?"

"Hey! You forget—I was doing this stuff when you were playing catch with Daddy in the backyard. There aren't too many places I can't get into."

Toma sat on the edge of the bed. "Johnny, things are happening fast and furious and we've gotta talk."

Reece pushed Toma's hand away and sat up. "Fast and furious, huh? Don't tell me, the senator's coming in today and not tomorrow."

Toma shook his head. "No, he'll still be here tomorrow."

"But Argari doesn't want me to take him out now, right? Hit or no hit, the deal is, I still get paid."

"You're jumping to a lot of conclusions, Johnny. It's very uncharacteristic of you. Nothing's changed." He paused and then continued, "No, everything's changed."

Toma smiled and went on to tell Reece of all that had happened during the night. Reece listened intently. When the story was over, he got out of bed, walked across his large one-room studio apartment to the refrigerator, took out a container of orange juice and poured himself a glass.

"No wonder you look so tired," Reece said. He drank some juice. "You've been a busy, busy boy."

Toma didn't say a word. Reece continued, "Let's see if I've got this correct. You hired Tinkerbell the Hitman to waste Kane. He blew it, so now Tinkerbell's dead and Kane's probably having breakfast at the hotel, even as we speak. You and Lauder tried to whack Caputo, and he's alive and well and camping somewhere out in the State Forest—but you tagged Lauder all by yourself. Although, if I remember correctly, he was on *our* side! Toma, do you know what the hell you're doing?"

"I know perfectly well what I'm doing. I'm trying to save our asses!"

"What?"

"On the surface, Argari looks calm and in control, but Johnny, take it from me, the damn guy's short circuiting." Toma sounded angry. "I've been with Argari for a long time. It's been a good ride, but I'm not going down with him. I've worked too hard to let him ruin it all for me now."

"Loyalty's an amazing thing," Reece said sarcastically.

"Originally, Argari's plan was to kill Kane separately. I didn't think anything of it. Then he got this brainstorm—he even called it 'Divine Intervention.' He wants to tie Kane into tomorrow's job."

"How?"

"I don't know how. I don't think Argari knows how. But he's not thinking with all his marbles anymore. You know what will happen if he screws this up? This is a major hit. The people who want the senator dead sit at the highest levels of government. Chicago promised them this would be clean and professional. If Argari blows it, they'll blow our heads off—and I mean *our* heads—yours and mine."

Reece finished the juice and placed the glass in the sink. "I have to admit that if the plan isn't executed properly—I mean, if everything doesn't go like clockwork, it won't work at all. This is, far and away, the riskiest assignment I've ever done."

"Did Argari mention anything to you about Kane?" Toma asked.

"Nope."

Toma started to tap his fingers on the night table. "The way I see it, there are now three major obstacles standing in the way and their names are Caputo, Kane and Argari."

"You really mean it, don't you? You're gonna get rid of Argari."

"They've *all* gotta go."

Reece walked over to the sofa and sat down. "You don't expect me to do them all and the senator too, do you?"

"I'll take care of Argari," Toma said without hesitation.

"You've got this thing all figured out, don't you?"

Toma answered, "I killed a cop last night. First there's gonna be a lot of questions and then they'll be watching me like a hawk. I'd never be able to get close enough to kill Kane or Caputo, never mind both of them."

"Why me? Why not one of your other creepy friends?" Reece asked.

"Your ass is at stake. You know they've gotta go as much as I do."

"And, of course, I don't get paid for any of this extra crap."

"No one gets paid. These are freebies" Toma said.

"I've never done a job I didn't get paid for," Reece said, with a wry smile. "I don't believe in killing for killing sake."

"Do you believe in life in prison? Do you believe in getting your head blown off by our friends in Chicago? I can assure you, Reece, one of those two things will happen to us if you don't help me take care of this." Toma was still nervously tapping his fingers.

"For crying out loud, stop that!" Reece yelled, pointing to Toma's hand. Toma stopped instantly. The two men took a moment to quietly think the situation over.

"Odds are Caputo's already talked to some people," Reece said.

"Yeah, well all they've got right now is his word and the bump on his head."

"You seem fairly certain they're not gonna arrest you."

Toma emphasized every word. "They've-got-to-find-a-body."

"What'd you do with it?"

"I gave it a hot steel bath." Toma laughed

"A what?"

"I dropped the body into a ladle of molten steel, at a mill on the South Side."

"No one saw you?" Reece sounded impressed.

"You spread a couple of hundred dollars around and everyone takes a coffee break. No one wants to know what you're doing. As far as they're concerned, it's just free money."

Reece smiled briefly. "And the body—it disintegrated, right?"

"Of course," Toma agreed.

"How about the car?" Reece continued.

Toma shook his head. "I pushed it into a slurry pond."

"What the hell's a slurry pond?"

"All the old mills have one. It's a huge vat of industrial acid—I mean the strong stuff. It's how they get rid of a lot of their waste materials. Ya drop a car in one of those and it dissolves like Alka Seltzer."

Toma was amused. “After a few weeks, they pour the liquefied remains into a slag dump, where it cools, hardens and remains forever as an indistinguishable mass of nothing.”

Toma stood and walked to the window. “No, without a body, they haven’t got a case.” He turned back to Reece. “For all they know, Lauder drove to Atlantic City, with some broad.”

Reece paused a second and then said, “No wonder you got as far as you did. You don’t miss a trick, Alonzo. I’d hate to get you pissed off at me.”

“You’re right. It wouldn’t be a good idea, Johnny.” There was a threatening tone in his voice.

“Okay. Get outta here and let me get dressed,” Reece said. “I’ve got a lot of work to do. If I’m gonna clip three people within forty-eight hours, and not get caught, I’ll have to put together a plan.”

“I wanna know what’s going on. We’ll need to talk again,” Toma said.

“Tonight, after the game, I’ll call your car phone—let’s say around eleven. We’ll decide on a place to meet.” Reece was all business.

Toma crossed the room to the door, took hold of the handle and stopped. “Hey Reece.”

Johnny looked up at Toma. “What?”

“It wouldn’t be wise to cross me. You may have the cutest ass in town—” Toma opened the door, took a step into the hall, turned and grinned. “But I’d kill you in a heartbeat.”

Reece raised his hands, as if surrendering. “Alonzo, baby, come on! We’re buddies.”

The door closed and Toma was gone.

“Up yours, you faggy bastard,” Reece said as he made an obscene gesture with his middle finger. He sat for a moment, absorbing all that had just taken place. “This is crazy,” he said.

Then he picked up the telephone and dialed a number that began with three-one-two—the Chicago area code.

Chapter Thirteen

Pittsburghers are proud of Point State Park. To them, it's a dramatic symbol of how much this dignified old steel town has changed. For most of Pittsburgh's history, dirty warehouses and rundown rail yards covered this location. But midway through the twentieth century, the caterpillar became a butterfly. The town fathers had called the transformation, "Renaissance I" and "Renaissance II."

The first Renaissance took place in the '50s and '60s; the second, in the '70s and '80s. They were enormous and ambitious periods of razing and rebuilding. An area that once had one of the worst pollution problems on the planet, instituted tough new controls, and soon its air was fresh and clean. Landmark buildings, long stained by black smoke, were scrubbed and sand-blasted. And the warehouses and rail yards at the very tip of the city, where the Monongahela meets the Allegheny to form the Ohio River, were removed and replaced with lawns, sidewalks and a wide assortment of beautiful trees. A mess had become a masterpiece. Pittsburgh—once a city that evoked snickers and bad jokes—had regained the respect and admiration of the world. And this neat little park definitely impressed Jack Kane.

Kane gave up on Caputo by ten-thirty and decided to take a short walk around The Point to clear the cobwebs. The time disappeared and the *short* walk stretched into a long hour-and-a-half. It was a beautiful day in a surprisingly lovely city, and it was easy for Kane to temporarily put aside the complicated Kaplan case. It was as he was walking out of the park and about to cross the street to the hotel, when he glanced up and noticed the plywood covering the window Meanny's body crashed through the night before. It all came rushing back. Kane remembered why he was there. He knew he had lots to do.

He maneuvered around the parked cars in front of the building, passed through the front door and into the hotel lobby. It seemed busier then usual.

Kane hadn't walked ten feet when he heard, "I thought you went back to New York!"

He turned and saw Caputo sitting in an easy chair. He looked harried and disheveled.

"What? You sleep in your cab last night? You look terrible," Kane said.

Caputo smiled. "This is how the style-conscious undercover cop dresses these days."

Then Kane saw the welt on the side of Caputo's face. "And *that* looks nice," he said sarcastically "You walk into a fist?"

Caputo smiled and then winced. "Aw, come on. It hurts to laugh." Caputo rubbed his cheek. "Sit down over here and I'll tell you the whole story."

Kane walked over and sat in a comfortable chair opposite Caputo. Just then an entourage consisting of six men and an attractive young woman walked into the lobby. It seemed that everyone in the room turned to look at them.

"Wonder who they are," Kane said.

"The elder statesman in the middle of the group is Senator Mike Mullen.

"You're kidding!" Kane was impressed. "A fellow mick."

Caputo smiled. "Yes, he's probably a patron saint of yours."

"You Catholic?"

"With a name like Caputo, what do you think?"

"You go to Catholic school?" Kane asked.

"Saint John the Baptist, for five years."

"Well didn't they tell you that you had to be die to become a saint?"

"I slept a lot in religion class."

Kane smiled, and then looked back at the senator. "How about the others?"

"Two of them are aides, and the other three—the ones with bulges in their coats—are body guards."

"He needs *three* body guards? What the hell for?"

"This is the senator who's asking all those questions about the Kennedy assassination."

Kane remembered." Of course. Mullen. He's the one who wants all the files made public."

"What he calls 'the real secret files.'" Caputo rubbed his eyes. He was tired. "Officially, the government says Mullen's talking through his hat."

"And unofficially?" Kane asked.

"Unofficially? Word on the street is a lot of people in power wouldn't be terribly upset if he were to die suddenly."

"That assassination stuff happened such a long time ago," Kane said.

"Well, Mullen says he's doing what he's doing because he wants to return honesty to government. He says our government's been living a lie for nearly forty years and it's time to come clean—for real."

"What do you think?"

"I think he's absolutely right." Caputo sounded serious.

"I do, too," Kane agreed. "Who's the young girl?"

"I'm not sure. I know it's not his wife. She died in a car crash two years ago. And he seems like too straight an arrow to be courting some young wench." Caputo started to laugh and winced again.

"Well anyway, you were going to tell me about how you got your wound," Kane said, turning back to Caputo.

Caputo closed his eyes, put both hands to his face and was quiet, as if gathering his thoughts. Then he took his hands away. If there was any humor in his expression before, now it was gone.

"You were right. Lauder was dirty."

"*Was* dirty?"

"He's dead. I saw Toma kill him last night."

For the next ten minutes, Kane listened to the young detective's story, riveted to his every word. Caputo finished his narrative with, "Something big's going down this weekend and I've gotta find out what it is before it happens."

"So, they murdered Kaplan in order to lure me to Pittsburgh." Kane shook his head. "That's a helluva reason for a man to die."

"It sure is," Caputo agreed.

"Where's Toma now?"

"I don't know. I do know there's no body, no blood, no proof of any of this. All I've got to show for last night is this bruise on my face, and *that* could have come from anywhere."

"You've been to Argari's?"

"First thing I did when I got back to the station was to take a couple of guys and go out there. He was very cooperative. He let us look everywhere. He said Mr. Toma had spent the entire night with his accountant and him, working on taxes. The accountant verified his story. But then, if Argari said they had been roping buffalo, the accountant would have gone along with that, too."

Kane smiled. "Where'd he say Toma was?"

"He said Toma was running a few errands."

"I'm sure he was," Kane inserted.

"And as soon as he returned, he said he'd make certain Mr. Toma gave us a call."

"How civic-minded of him," Kane said. "If it's any consolation, I believe you."

"Thank you."

"So, Kaplan and I are one thing, and this big job, this weekend, is another."

"And Toma's pissed because Argari wanted to tie the two together."

"How inconsiderate." Kane ran his hand along his beard. "You have to admit, Argari's got a lot of guts. I mean, he knows he's gonna be watched, yet you know he's still going ahead with whatever it is."

"The way they were talking last night, it's big and there'll be no second chances," Caputo said. "They've got to go ahead with it."

Then Caputo looked across the room and saw the senator's young lady friend smiling at him. He was quick to return the smile.

"I thought you were married," Kane said, noticing Caputo's action.

"Nope. I tell people I am when I'm undercover. It adds meat to the story, but in real life I haven't met the right girl yet."

"Your story, huh? That reminds me, all that stuff you told me when you were driving me in from the airport—all bullshit, right?"

"You mean what I told you about the kidnappers of that poor kid? Most of that was true."

"What wasn't?" Kane asked.

"Well, my partner wasn't shot because I was alone when I found the kidnappers. The part about the pictures was true except, I broke into the room about a minute before the husband was gonna do the kid."

Caputo seemed less comfortable telling the real story. "The kid was naked, the man's pants were off, and the wife was sticking a sock into the kid's mouth. It wasn't a pretty picture. The poor little girl's mind and body had been raped. First thing I did was shoot the husband right in the balls. Instant castration. I thought it was unintentional, but the more I thought about it afterward, the more I realized—I had aimed. While he was rolling around, holding a hole where his pecker used to be, the wife pulled a .25 caliber. But before she could do anything with it, I shot her in the forehead—killed her instantly. I looked at the terrified little girl, then the pig on the floor—and I shot him again. It was wrong. I never should have done that. It was too quick. I let him off too easy. What I should have done is let him bleed to death."

"I take it no one fired you." Kane said.

"Fired me? Hell, they gave me a medal and a promotion. As for the kid—she's catatonic—hasn't said a word to anybody since. It happened over two years ago. I stop by and see her all the time, but she doesn't know I'm there. They don't know if she'll ever come out of it."

"Damn shame."

"That, my friend, is an understatement," Caputo said, as if coming out of a trance.

He looked back at the young woman standing by the senator, but she had turned her attention to the desk clerk. He admired her for a moment or two.

Kane's voice brought him back to reality. "Hey Tom, your love life's gonna have to wait. We got some bad guys to catch."

Caputo turned back to Kane and he had a serious look on his face. "Jack, you're not a cop anymore. You can't get involved in this."

"I'm already involved. A friend's dead and Toma's tried to have me taken out. Either I'm in with you or I'm in without you, but I guarantee you, I'm in."

Caputo knew Kane was right. There was no dealing him out of the game now. He had a hand and he was going to play it.

"You're stubborn, Kane."

"It's the Irish in me," Kane said with a smile.

"Yeah, well my grandmother was Irish and she wasn't as stubborn as you."

"Caputo, you had an Irish grandmother?"

"Mary O'Reilly was her name."

"I knew there was something I liked about you," Kane said.

Once again, Caputo glanced at the young woman. "Jack, she's a fine looking woman."

Kane looked over his shoulder at her. "Yeah, but she's a thoroughbred. She wouldn't have anything to do with a mongrel like you."

He turned to Caputo. "Well, come on! We've got things to do."

Just as the two men stood up, Johnny Reece entered the hotel. He walked directly to the senator.

"Senator Mullen?" Reece asked, extending his hand.

The senator shook his hand but anyone could clearly see from the expression on his face that the senator didn't know Reece.

Reece continued, "I'm from the Pirates, Senator. My name's Johnny Reece."

The Senator's face lit up. The young woman looked excited to see him, too.

"Johnny Reece! Why you're a household name around the Mullen home. We've been fans from the beginning, isn't that right, Susan?" he asked his young female companion.

Kane recognized Reece as soon as he had heard his voice. He and Caputo watched from across the room.

"My father's absolutely correct. Living in Washington, you'd think we would be Orioles fans, but Dad's been following the Bucs since he was a kid. I was weaned on the Pirates. If we weren't talking politics, we were talking baseball—the Maz, Stargel, Clemente."

"And you seem to be carrying on the tradition, Mr. Reece," the senator said.

"Please, Senator, call me Johnny."

Mullen took Reece by the arm. "We've just finished checking in. My aides are going to take our bags up to the room. We were going to go into the dinning room for a bite to eat—we'd love to have you join us."

"Gee Senator, I don't want to impose."

Susan smiled at Reece. Caputo noticed and felt jealous.

"You wouldn't be an imposition, Mr. Reece."

Reece looked into Susan's beautiful blue eyes and smiled. "It would be my pleasure."

Then he looked over at Kane and Caputo and grinned.

"The bastard's rubbing it in," Caputo said angrily.

"Nah—he's just busting *my* balls. He doesn't even know you," Kane replied.

Caputo and Reece glared at each other for a moment. There was a gleam of amusement in the athlete's eyes

"Don't kid yourself, Jack. He knows me," Caputo said.

The senator, Susan and Reece walked into the dining room and were gone.

"Let's get back to business," Kane said.

"What do you think our next move should be?" Caputo asked.

"Let's keep the pressure on Argari." Kane answered as he started for the door. "You're driving."

Caputo followed. "You know, I'm starting to feel like a damned cab driver."

The cab was parked in a no-parking space, just down the street from the cab stand. When the two men arrived, there was a ticket stuck under the wiper. Caputo grabbed it from the windshield.

"Damn meter maids! They're a real pain in the ass. If they knew what they were doing, they would have checked the plates and realized this was a police vehicle."

Kane smiled. "I wouldn't pay it, if I were you."

"Yeah, right. Just get into the car." Caputo tossed the citation onto the back seat and got in. Kane sat on the passenger side.

"You always leave your car unlocked?" Kane asked.

"Bad habit. I never locked the cruiser when I was in uniform, and I keep forgetting to do it now."

He keyed the ignition, put it in gear and pulled away from the curb.

"Man, I can't get that girl outta my head! She's beautiful."

"Yeah, I can see her leaving her aristocratic environment to become a cop's wife," Kane said, shaking his head.

They turned the corner onto Fort Duquesne Boulevard and passed the big red KDKA radio and TV sign.

"You think it would be too much of a sacrifice?" Caputo was playing along. "Don't you think I'm worth it?"

"Well I haven't known you very long.—"

"Just a few days," Caputo inserted.

"Less, if we're talking about the *real* you and not your cover. But are you worth it? In my opinion, I'd have to say no."

Caputo laughed as he pulled an illegal U turn and steered the cab up the ramp toward the Fort Duquesne Bridge. The rapidly changing weather, with its fluctuating temperatures, has always reeked havoc on the roads of western Pennsylvania. In this part of the world, potholes are as common as stop signs. Caputo's cab nailed a big one, as they started across the bridge. The briefcase fell off the backseat and onto the floor. Kane reached over, picked it up and put it back.

"Hope you don't have anything valuable in there," he said.

Caputo looked into his rearview mirror and then back to the road.

"What are you talking about?"

"Your briefcase! I hope you don't have anything valuable in your briefcase," Kane repeated.

"I don't have a briefcase."

Kane looked back at the case. Instantly, he knew what it was. "Pull over to the side!" he yelled.

Caputo still wasn't sure what was happening. "On the bridge?" he asked.

"Yes, now! On the bridge."

Caputo cut the wheel hard to the right and slammed on the brakes. The car fishtailed to a quick stop. Kane jumped out and pulled open the back door.

"Get out—quick!" he screamed at Caputo.

Caputo didn't waste any time. He did exactly as ordered. Kane picked up the briefcase and lifted it out of the cab, careful not to bump it against anything. Then, he gingerly carried it to the bridge railing, praying, with each step that it wouldn't blow up in his face. He leaned back and, with the form of a discus thrower, flung it over the side. Just as he released it, he noticed a huge coal barge, passing below.

"Damn!"

He watched the case descend, tumbling end over end. It seemed to fall forever. He thought it would explode close to the bridge deck, but it didn't. The farther away it fell, the more he thought that maybe it wasn't a bomb after all. It was possible he had thrown away someone's misplaced business valise.

Then, it hit the top of a large pile of coal and detonated with the force of ten sticks of dynamite. Chunks of ore flew everywhere—some shooting higher than the bridge, and a few narrowly missing Kane's face. Even though he expected it, the size of the explosion surprised him. By the time he had dropped for cover, the danger had passed.

Kane got back up and leaned over the railing, but the barge had slipped under the bridge and passed from view. He turned and saw that Caputo had already crossed the four lanes to the other side.

"Is everyone alright?" Caputo yelled to some crewmembers below. He listened for a moment and then continued, "We'll get a boat right out to you."

Then he took a small hand-held two-way from his coat pocket and relayed the details to headquarters. He turned to look back at the cab and was surprised to find Kane standing right behind him.

"You okay?" Caputo asked.

"Scared the daylights outta me. I'm still shaking," Kane said.

"You think it frightened you, how would you have liked to have been down there?" Caputo pointed to the vessel below. "They won't forget that for awhile."

"Anyone hurt?"

"I don't think so. I don't see any bodies floating in the water. No one's screaming for help."

"How comforting," Kane said

"Relax! It landed on a coal heap, on the front barge. Looks like most of the crew was on the tug, three lengths back. The explosion made a lot of noise and blew a bunch of coal into the Allegheny. The crew will be washing their underwear tonight, but that's about it."

Just then, a police boat came around The Point from the Mon River side, and signaled the barge tug with a blast from its air horn.

"Ah, reinforcements have arrived," Caputo said.

*　*　*　*

The bang was loud enough to shake windows and rattle dishes in the hotel dining room. Reece smiled as soon as he heard it, then he sipped some wine. Susan signaled the manager and he hurried over to the table.

"Did something happen in the hotel?" she asked.

"No, Miss. I believe that sound came from somewhere near the stadium," he replied.

"Probably Brian Giles hitting batting practice," the senator said, with a laugh.

Reece smiled again, acknowledging the senator's flimsy attempt at humor, and took another mouthful of Zinfandel.

Chapter Fourteen

Kane never realized how boring it was to hang around in the hallway of a police station. For more than three hours—or two cups of coffee and one partially melted candy bar—the old New York cop had been waiting for Caputo to return from the bowels of the building with word on what the lab boys had found on the barge and in the cab. He had to smile when it occurred to him that most of the characters walking in and out of the precinct were similar, in so many ways, to people he remembered from his days working the old 25th, back in the Apple.

Then there was a tap on his shoulder. He turned to an unsmiling Caputo.

"Don't tell me. They didn't find anything," Kane said.

"Right."

"No fingerprints in the car or on the case?"

"No fingerprints in the car, and the briefcase disintegrated. If there were any pieces left, they're heading down the Ohio and are halfway to Cincinnati by now."

"Damn!" Kane said. "You know it has to be Argari."

Caputo shook his head. "Who knows? It could be the reincarnation of Lucky Luciano for all we know. We've got nothing. Everything's circumstantial."

Kane banged the wall with his fist. "I know it's that bastard. Twice in less then twenty-four hours someone tries to hit me and the only people I know in this town are you and that crazy son of a bitch."

Caputo smiled. "And I give tourists at least a week before I take a contract out on them."

"Cute." Kane smiled back. "Listen, we've gotta sit Mr. Argari down again and have a little talk with him."

"I know." Caputo said.

"And I think we should do it right now."

"I agree."

"Well, let's go!" Kane said impatiently.

"Go where?"

"To Argari's!"

"We don't have to."

"What do you mean we don't have to?"

"Because he's sitting in the next room." Caputo pointed to a door not more than six feet away that had the word "Interrogation" stenciled on it.

"I didn't see you bring him in!" Kane sounded surprised.

"There's a back entrance," Caputo told him.

"Oh! Well, that makes sense," Kane said.

The first thing Kane noticed when he walked into the room was that Argari was obviously uneasy. Kane couldn't help but feel good about this. Every other time they had met, the gangster looked confident and in control. Now, his eyes moved constantly like those of a caged animal, and he shifted around in his seat as if it were impossible for him to find a comfortable position. The room was dark, except for one bright light.

Kane turned to Caputo. "Looks like a set from an old Jimmy Cagney movie." Kane whispered his best Cagney impersonation to Caputo. "Talk, youuuu dirt-yyy raaatt."

"What can I say? My captain's a very dramatic person," Caputo said.

* * * *

Argari heard the mumbling in the darkness and looked in their direction. "I don't know what the hell's going on here, but if I don't get to speak to my lawyer pretty damned soon, someone's gonna be in deep shit," Argari screamed.

Kane stepped out of the darkness, followed by Caputo.

Argari recognized him immediately. "Son of a bitch! I should have known you'd be behind this."

Caputo was the first to speak. "I'd like to thank you for voluntarily coming down to talk with us, Mr. Argari. We deeply appreciate your cooperation."

"Voluntarily, my ass. You had me picked up like a common criminal."

"Oh, and Caputo, my friend, Mr. Argari is anything but a *common* criminal," Kane said, as he pulled up a chair and sat down.

"We only have a few quick questions, Mr. Argari," Caputo began.

Kane interrupted, "Yeah, like why'd you plant a bomb in Detective Caputo's car a few hours ago?"

Argari looked legitimately surprised. "I don't know what you're talking about! I don't have a beef with Detective Caputo."

"Oh? Well who *do* you have a beef with?" Kane asked.

"In my line of work, you run into many people who give you a hard time."

"Is that so," Caputo said.

"Yes, but I've been around a long time." Argari looked over at Kane. "And I can handle it."

"Just like you handled Kaplan?" Kane continued.

"Haven't we been through this before, Kane? I told you I had nothing to do with—" He smiled. "That unfortunate incident."

Kane fought to control his anger.

"And what line of work are you in, Mr. Argari?" Caputo asked

"I'm in the import-export business. It's very cutthroat."

Kane looked over at Caputo. "Cutthroat! Well, he's well qualified."

"Detective Caputo, if I'm supposed to be here *voluntarily* then I should be able to leave whenever I want, is that correct?"

Caputo looked at Kane and then back to Argari. "Yes, that's correct."

"Well then, I want to leave now."

Argari stood up but Kane pushed him back into his seat.

"Hey! What the hell's going on here?" Argari yelled. "I'm gonna have your badge, Caputo, for allowing this retired New York sleeze bag to rough me up."

Caputo took Kane by the arm and walked him into the darkness to confer. "Easy, Jack. You're gonna get us both in trouble," Caputo whispered.

"Give me two minutes alone with Argari."

"What!"

"I won't hurt him. I won't touch him. I just want to give him something to think about."

Caputo thought for a moment. "You better just talk to him. I'm trusting you, Kane. Don't let me down or I'll toss your ass in jail."

Caputo turned and walked out. Argari squinted his eyes, trying to see who had entered or left the room. Kane stepped into the light once again. Argari slumped back in his seat.

"So, what are you gonna do? Break out the rubber hose and beat the crap outta me?"

Kane smiled. "Sounds good to me."

Argari's eyes got big. It was the first time Kane had ever seen them filled with fear.

Kane sat in the chair again. "Relax, Argari. Only the bad guys do stuff like that."

"Yeah, right." Argari snapped back.

"Well, maybe I am exaggerating a bit. I guess a few on our team have done it on occasion."

"Like you," Argari said.

"Maybe when I was younger," Kane agreed. "But I promised my friend I'd be a good boy, and I never break a promise."

Kane rubbed his beard. He was feeling tired. The turmoil of the last few days was starting to wear on him. "Argari, I'm not stupid enough to think you're gonna give me any straight answers today. For that matter, I know you're not gonna give me any answers at all."

"You got that right." Argari snickered.

"So, before you leave, I'm gonna give you a few things to ponder."

"I'm all ears."

"I think—no, make that, I *know* you killed Kaplan. You did it because you've hated him for years and you knew he was a friend of mine. Killing him would get me here. You wanted me in unfamiliar territory. Am I right so far?"

Argari simply smiled and said nothing.

"You know what they say, 'Silence speaks louder than words.'"

"The expression is, '*Actions* speak louder than words'—and I live by it," Argari said forcefully.

"Ah! I just wanted to see if you're paying attention." Kane grinned. "I must admit, I haven't got the whole thing figured out, but if you didn't have the bomb planted and if you didn't try to have me aced last night, then I'd have to say that there's a renegade in your tribe. You've got a loose cannon rolling around your deck."

Argari looked away from Kane, but the detective continued, "If I were in your shoes and someone was making decisions like that without my knowledge or approval, I'd be concerned. You see, I'd start to think that whoever that someone is—well, it sounds like they're not gonna want to take orders from you much longer." Kane got up again. "If I were you Argari, I'd sleep with the door locked and a pistol under my pillow."

Just then Caputo came back into the room.

"I always do, Kane," Argari responded.

Caputo switched on the main overhead light.

"Mr. Argari, thank you for your help. You can go now," Caputo said.

The gangster got up and walked to the door. "Caputo! What's a nice Italian boy like you doing hanging around an Irish scumbag like Kane?"

Caputo smiled. "Learning how to put slime balls like you in jail."

Argari glared at the cop for a second and then walked out of the room, slamming the door behind him.

Kane patted Caputo on the shoulder. "You keep that up and maybe someday you'll be as loved by the underworld as I am."

Kane walked to the door. "Let's go," he said.

"Now where?" Caputo asked.

"I've planted the seed. Let's see if it grows."

Kane left the room, followed by Caputo who turned off the lights on the way out.

* * * *

Reece had spent the entire afternoon with the senator and his daughter. At first, Susan thought the ballplayer was attractive and someone she'd like to know better. But the more he talked, the more he turned her off. His conversation was limited to baseball and hunting. It wasn't the baseball that bothered her. She was a fan and could tolerate that. It was his enthusiastic endorsement of a practice she despised—hunting. That made her sick to her stomach. She was a staunch supporter of animal rights, and he was the enemy. The senator listened politely, as most any good politician would, while Reece described the thrill he got from stalking wild animals, killing them and then gutting the carcasses himself. After awhile, the young woman could take no more. She asked to be excused, saying that she was suffering side effects from a bad case of the flu that she had two weeks before. As she left the table, the senator smiled. He knew that she hadn't had the flu.

"I hope she's alright," Reece said as he watched her leave the room.

"Oh, she's strong. I'm sure it'll pass," said the senator.

"All things do." Reece smiled across the table at the Senator. "So, where will you be sitting at tomorrow's game, Senator?"

"I wanted to be right down in the front row, but the security people said that I'd be safer in a private box."

"Sounds like you've got more security around you than the President," Reece commented.

"Well, I guess I've raised a few eyebrows with my work involving the Kennedy assassination. My security people have heard that there's a contract out on me. Can you believe that?" The senator laughed.

"You? How ridiculous," Reece said with a slight smile.

"Well, after next week, everything should be alright," Mullen continued.

"What's next week?" Reece asked.

"I will have spoken in front in Congress and certain wheels will be in motion. It'll be out of my hands and left to the nation to decide. Once the people know what's going on, the cat will be out of the bag, so to speak, and my death will be unnecessary."

"Ah, well I would think the last place your security people would want you to be, right now, is at a ball park with fifty thousand people around you."

The senator laughed again. "You've got that right. But I'm a very hard man to put down, Mr. Reece. I don't like being made a prisoner by a bunch of raving lunatics."

"I don't blame you one bit, Senator. I'd feel the same way, if I were you."

"So, tomorrow I'll be safely tucked away in the VIP box above home plate, watching you pitch your first no-hitter." He smiled.

"I wouldn't hold my breath, if I were you, Sir," Reece said. "The VIP box, huh? You'll have a great view of the game."

"I hope so."

"I'll be able to look right up at you from the mound. Why, if things get boring, you can give me the signals instead of Lavalliare."

"A sure way for you to lose the game," said the senator, as he got up from the table. "I'm afraid I've got a bunch of work to do, back in my suite. It's been a pleasure spending the afternoon with you, Mr. Reece."

"I've enjoyed it too, Senator." Reece stood as he shook Mullen's hand. "Again, extend my regrets to your daughter. Tell her I wish her a speedy recovery."

"She'll be fine. Good luck tomorrow."

"I'll give it my best shot." Reece smiled. "If I get a chance, I'll stop up and see you."

"I'd like that. Hey, maybe we'll get lucky and you'll get a homerun for us tomorrow."

"I don't know about a homerun, but you can count on a hit."

"I'll look forward to it," Mullen said, just before he turned and walked away from the table.

Reece watched him leave the room, laughed to himself, then sat down and ordered another glass of wine.

* * * *

"Where the hell's this guy going?" Caputo asked Kane.

Kane sat quietly on the passenger side of their car intently watching the vehicle in front of them maneuver Pittsburgh's complicated terrain.

"You know, Jack, I don't think he knows where he's going," Caputo said.

"Whatever I said must've hit home."

"If he were going to his place, he'd be headed in the opposite direction."

Just then Argari steered his car into the parking lot of a large townhouse complex. He drove past two buildings and stopped in front of the third.

"Well, what have we here?" Caputo asked.

"Could be a safe house," Kane said. "Maybe this is where our friend Toma is hanging out these days."

Caputo stopped in an empty driveway, just up the road from Argari. The Pittsburgh detective reached under the front seat and took out a pair of Zeiss glasses.

Kane nodded his approval. "I like a man who comes prepared. I bet when you were a kid, you always had a safe in your wallet, too."

Caputo smiled and then turned his attention to Argari who walked up the stairs, fumbled with some keys, unlocked the front door and entered the townhouse without knocking.

"Well, either it's his or he's real good friends with the owner because he just walked right in," Caputo said as he continued to look through the glasses.

"You mind?" Kane reached for the binoculars.

"Be my guest." Caputo handed them to him.

Argari wasn't inside five minutes. Suddenly, he came storming out of the building, got into his car and drove off quickly.

"Do we follow him?" Caputo asked.

"I'd sure like to know what's in that apartment," said Kane. "It's a gamble, but I'd bet he's headed back to his house. I think we'll be able to catch up with him there."

"I'll need a warrant to get into this place," Caputo said, pointing toward the condo.

"I won't." Kane grinned.

Caputo was about to protest but Kane raised his hand. "Tell you what. Why don't you rest you eyes for a few minutes—I know you're tired. I'll go for a little stroll. Just don't open your eyes until I get back."

Caputo knew exactly what Kane was about to do. "Talk about stretching the law," he said.

Kane pretended to be shocked. "Why Detective Caputo, I don't know what you're talking about!"

Before another word could be spoken, Kane was out of the car and on his way. Caputo couldn't keep his eyes closed. He took the glasses again and watched his friend walk to the front door, knock and then wait for a response. A moment later, he rang the bell. Still, there was no answer. Then he saw Kane take something from his jacket pocket and push it into the door's lock. It opened easily. Kane stepped inside, turned to Caputo, waved, smiled and closed the door.

"You crazy bastard. We'll be cellmates," Caputo said.

* * * *

The townhouse was sparsely furnished. There were no pictures or decorations—just the basic essentials—table, chairs, sofa, and a couple of beds in the two rooms upstairs. It didn't take him long to determine that he was the only person in the house. The search was simple. Most of the closets were empty—all except for the one at the top of the stairs. There, he found some clothes, a small suitcase and—taped inside one of the shoes—a key to a locker.

"Well, what's this?"

He peeled off the tape and examined it closely. "What secrets are you hiding?"

He was about to put the expensive shoe back when he noticed something engraved on the inside heel: "A. TOMA."

"Home away from home," Kane said.

He made another quick look around. There was nothing else. He had seen all that was to be seen.

* * * *

As quickly as he had entered, Kane was out and a minute or two later, sitting in the car next to Caputo.

"What'd you find?"

"I was right. It's a safe house. Sort of the bad guy's Motel 6."

"So that's where Toma's hiding," Caputo concluded.

"Bingo! But, as I'm sure you've already figured out, he's not there now. I mean, if he had been home, I seriously doubt that he would have let me search his closet or take this key that I found taped inside one of his shoes. I can't imagine him being that accommodating, can you?"

Caputo smiled. "No, I don't think so."

"My good man, to the bus station." Kane said dramatically. "We've a locker to open."

Caputo started the car, pulled it into gear and executed an incredibly sloppy U turn, turfing part of the development's lawn in the process.

"I hope no one gets your license plate number," said Kane.

"That's the least of our problems," Caputo answered, referring to the breaking and entering.

Caputo swerved the car back onto the main road and sped away in the direction of the city.

Chapter Fifteen

Argari was fuming. The drive back to his South Hills estate couldn't go fast enough. He knew that much of what Kane had said was true. Someone was acting without his knowledge or approval. He also knew that, the someone had to Toma.

"For years, I trusted you, you rotten bastard," he yelled, pounding the steering wheel. "When I get my hands on you—" He didn't finish the sentence. He didn't have to.

The front gates opened with a remote control and Argari was pressing the button long before he came into range. It was fortunate that they opened quickly, otherwise he would have driven his car right through them. His automobile screeched to a stop in front of the estate's main entrance, and one of his goons hurried to open his car door.

"Is Toma here?" he barked.

He was already through the front door before the man could answer. His footsteps echoed on the marble foyer floor. The front door hadn't closed behind him, when he noticed a light on in his private study.

"Son of a bitch!" he yelled.

He kicked the door with his foot and it swung open, hitting the wall behind it with a loud *bang!*

Argari's large desk chair was turned so he couldn't see who was sitting in it. But he didn't have to. He knew.

"How's it feel?" he said, suppressing rage.

Toma turned the chair in Argari's direction.

"The chair!" Argari continued. "How's it feel? You think you're big enough to fill it now?"

Toma smiled confidently. "I have been for years, my old friend."

Argari walked to one of the study's bookshelves, turned and leaned against it.

"So this is what it comes down to—you and me—a fight to the finish."

"Oh, I wouldn't say that, Argari. They'll be no fighting. We're both getting too old for that, and besides, I abhor violence."

"How sophisticated," Argari said sarcastically.

"A man in my newfound position must start thinking that way, don't you agree?" Toma said.

"And what position is that?" Argari asked.

"Why, the head of this organization," he answered.

"And what do you intend to do with me?" Argari asked.

Toma raised a pistol from his lap. "Well, you'll have to admit, two people can't do the same job. Seeing that I have the gun, I'd have to come to the conclusion that you lose."

"You would!" Argari spoke calmly, now.

"Come now Argari, even a pompous ass like you—someone as out of touch as you are—must see that I'm holding the ace." He nodded toward his weapon.

There was a large high-back chair between Argari and Toma, making it possible for Argari to slip his hand into one of the open slots on the book shelf without Toma seeing him do it. The expression on his face didn't change at all as he gripped the concealed Walther.

"You're gonna do it right here? Right now?" Argari asked.

"Right here. Right now," Toma responded. Then he pulled back the hammer and cocked the pistol. "I wish I could say that it's been fun, but I can't. Good-bye Argari, you no-good mother—"

Argari pulled the concealed weapon and fired before Toma could finish the sentence, never mind squeeze the trigger. The bullet hit Toma in the left eye and ripped out that whole side of his head. The pistol Toma was holding, fell to the floor and discharged on impact, harmlessly blowing a small hole in the ceiling. Before the smoke had cleared from Argari's gun barrel, two of his men were standing in the doorway, guns drawn.

"Gentlemen, I seem to have caused a mess here. I'd appreciate your cleaning it up and disposing of this." He pointed to the body. "This waste."

He put the gun down on the shelf and started to walk toward the door. "I'll be taking a shower."

* * * *

Pittsburgh built its bus station in the early '60s, and the community looked upon it as a shining example of what the city could be. The building was architecturally advanced and considered by many to be the first step in the town's transformation from steel furnace to sleek sophistication. It wasn't long before people realized that it was a step, but in the wrong direction. Almost from the start, it became a den for drug dealers, perverts and other societal lowlife. Before long, a visitor could find more lowlifes occupying space in that building than legitimate bus travelers. When the newness wore off, the building became tarnished and dirty. Much of it fell into disrepair. Respectable people either avoided going there or kept their visits short. The jewel had become junk.

Caputo shook his head when he pointed out the building to Kane. They were pulling up to the main entrance. "You know, you can't say too many good things about this place."

Caputo thought for a moment. "No, I take that back. You can't say *anything* good about this place."

Kane smiled. "I don't care what you say, it's urban renewal compared to the Port Authority in New York. People come here to sleep—they go *there* to die."

"I wouldn't want to take a short nap here either," Caputo continued.

The two men got out of the car and Caputo stuck a "Police Vehicle" sign on the dashboard before shutting and locking the doors.

"Glad you put that sign up." Kane grinned as he looked at the bums hanging around the steps. "You wouldn't want there to be any air in your tires when you got back."

"Don't laugh. I know most of these lovely people. They know that if they touch this car, I'll touch their heads with a riot stick."

"Ah, a man loved and respected by all who know him."

"If I wanted love and respect, I'd have become a priest like my brother."

Walking into the building was like stepping into a time warp. The improvements had stopped the day the contractor completed construction. The molded plastic seats were the same. The wall tiles were the same. The neon lighting was the same, as were the individual pay TVs, the foul-smelling bathrooms the lockers.

"What a dump," Caputo said.

"Hey, we're not here scouting locations for *Lifestyles of the Rich and Famous.*"

"Right. The lockers are over here," Caputo said, as he walked to a dark corner of the building.

"Why didn't they just put them in the basement?" Kane said sarcastically.

"What's the number again?"

Kane looked at the key. "Sixty-one."

Caputo looked around until he found the box. "Sixty-one. Here it is."

Kane tried to stick the key into the lock, but it didn't fit. "This can't be," he said. "The damn thing won't go in."

"Sounds like a line I said once on a date." Caputo laughed.

Kane didn't appreciate his humor. "Funny. If this doesn't work, we're back to ground zero."

Caputo took the key. "Here, let me try it. Maybe it needs the touch of an Italian craftsman." His luck was no better then Kane's.

All the while, an old drifter, sitting in the corner, watched the two men struggle. After a few minutes, he got up and shuffled over to them. "What seems to be the problem?"

Caputo looked at the man. "No problem. It's police business."

He tried the key again. Still nothing. The man stood quietly to one side.

"Let me try it again," Kane said taking the key. He looked at the number again to make sure it was correct. "Yup! Sixty-one, alright." He pushed it in, but it still wouldn't move.

The stranger moved closer. "Ya mind if I give it a shot?"

Caputo was about to brush him off, but Kane spoke first. "You think you can do better?"

The bum smiled. "I can't do any worse than you two."

Kane looked at Caputo and smiled. He looked back at the man. "Well, you've got something there."

He handed him the key. The old man examined the number, smiled and moved down to another box. He flipped the key over, slipped it into the lock and turned it. The lock released. He was about to pull the door open, when Kane slammed his hand against it, to keep it closed.

"Thank you very much." He turned to Caputo. "My friend here's got something for you."

Caputo thought for a second. "Oh, yeah. Here." he handed the man a five-dollar bill. Thanks for your time."

The old man took the cash turned and walked back to the corner.

"We're a couple of sharp detectives aren't we? We can't tell the difference between nineteen and sixty-one."

Caputo noticed Kane's hand on the door. "Well, aren't you gonna open it?"

Kane turned to the cop. "You got a small penlight?"

"Yeah, sure," Caputo said, taking one from his coat pocket and handing it to Kane. "What's the problem?"

Kane pulled the door open about a quarter of an inch, pointed the flashlight inside and looked in.

"Just as I thought. Some things about that Toma just never change."

He took a small knife from his pants pocket, opened the blade and peeled something away from the door.

"What's that?"

"Duct tape," Kane answered as he opened it the rest of the way. "Take a look for yourself."

Caputo looked inside and saw a black hand grenade the size of a baseball taped to the back of the locker. A small section of coat hanger was hooked around the pin with the opposite end taped to the door.

"Let's say you're some poor unsuspecting slob. You don't know what you're doing. You open the door, the wire pulls the pin on the grenade and you and the contents of this locker go bye-bye," Kane said, as he untaped the grenade and removed it from the locker. He checked the handle to make certain the pin was secure and handed it to Caputo. "Here, add this to your collection."

"Oh, I've got a bunch of these lying around the house," Caputo said taking the explosive with one hand and clicking on his portable two-way with the other. It only took a few seconds for him to request the bomb disposal unit.

"Good idea," Kane said. "We hit one of Pittsburgh's famous pot holes with that thing in the car, and we might go airborne."

"I never take unnecessary chances," said Caputo.

"Not true." Kane was looking inside the locker. "You're working a case with me, aren't you?"

"I stand corrected."

Kane continued, "You see, back in New York, Toma made a name for himself by doing just this thing. He was a master at booby-traps and car bombs. You wanted it gone, you called Toma. He'd blow it up for you."

"Sounds like a real fun guy."

"The life of any party. I'll tell you how good he was. We think he was responsible for at least a hundred of these things, and we couldn't prove that he did a single one."

"Slick. Why'd he stop?"

"He became Argari's right-hand man. When you're that high up in the organization, you just don't do stuff like that. That's what they pay other lowlife to do."

Kane shined the penlight light into the locker again, expecting to find something big and bulky, like a large folder or a package. He was disappointed.

"What the hell is *this?*" he said as he took out a small letter-size envelope. He could tell there was something hard inside.

"Rip it open and let's see," Caputo said.

"Not so fast. There's something solid in there. It might be a letter bomb."

"That size?"

Kane looked at Caputo and smiled. "That's why they call them letter bombs, my good man."

He felt around the perimeter of the envelope for a small wire, string or possibly a thread.

"Anything?"

"Not yet. Let's see if we can find a good-sized flashlight."

The two men walked to the main desk and asked an attendant to summon a security guard. After a few minutes, a large black man in his early forties arrived. Caputo recognized him immediately.

"Joe Trumbell!!"

"Caputo, you crazy bastard! How the hell are you?"

"I'm fine." he answered, shaking the guard's hand enthusiastically. "Question is, what the hell are you doing here?"

Trumbell shrugged his shoulders.

"A man's gotta feed his family."

"I thought you were working the South Side."

"I was, until about nine months ago. Then me and the force came to a parting of the ways."

"You're one of the best! What the hell could you have done wrong?"

Trumbell paused. Caputo could tell that the man didn't like rehashing the story.

"Hey, it's none of my business, man. I—"

Trumbell interrupted, "No, it's okay. You're a friend. I should've called you months ago."

Kane listened quietly while Trumbell continued, "They said I killed a kid when I didn't have to. They said it wasn't a *righteous* shooting. The punk had just killed a man in a convenience store and had pistol-whipped a teenage girl. His companion said the kid was getting ready to throw out the gun. The Board of

Inquiry took the word of a convicted felon over my testimony. I've been on the force for seventeen years man! I've got—I *had*—a great record. They said I wasn't in control of the situation. They suspended me without pay for six months. I told them to shove the job up their ass."

Caputo turned to Kane. "Typical. They push the good guys out and keep the assholes."

Kane smiled. "Assholes like to be around other assholes. They feel more comfortable. Talented, intelligent people intimidate them."

Caputo turned back to Trumbell. "Joe Trumbell—Jack Kane, NYPD retired."

The two men shook hands.

"Why are you two slumming down here?" Then he noticed the grenade in Caputo's hand. "And what the hell is that?"

Caputo did a quick synopsis of what had transpired.

"That's why we need *that,*" Kane said, pointing to Trumbell's flashlight.

"No problem," he said, handing it over.

Kane held the flashlight to the back of the letter. "Looks okay to me."

He handed the flashlight back to Trumbell and, without hesitation, tore open the envelope. It surprised Caputo, and he winced.

"Jumpy, aren't we?" said Kane.

"Little bit," Caputo admitted

Kane flipped the envelope upside down, and an unlabeled three-and-a-half-inch computer disk fell into his hand.

"Oh great!" Kane was disgusted. "You know anything about these things? I can't even operate my VCR, never mind run a computer."

"Well." Caputo hesitated. "Not really. The lab may be able to tell us something."

Trumbell laughed. "At this hour on a Saturday? Fat chance."

"He's right," Caputo agreed. "We might be able to get someone in on Sunday, but realistically, it probably won't get looked at until Monday morning."

"This is important stuff," Kane said. "You don't booby trap a Nintendo game card. Someone's gotta be able to help us before Monday."

"Ronny might be able to help you," Trumbell suggested.

Caputo recognized the name immediately. "Is he still into this stuff?"

"Is the Pope Catholic? He's got more computers than the Pentagon."

Kane was in the dark. "Ronny who?"

"Ronny is Joe's boy."

Anyone could see that Trumbell was proud of his son.

"He's a senior at Central Catholic. He's going to Penn State next year to major in engineering."

"Main campus?" Caputo asked.

"You got it, brother, and he's got a football scholarship, too."

Caputo held his hand out. "All right!" He slapped his friend's palm. "Of course, he gets his football ability from his old man."

"I'd like to think so."

"When can Ronny look at this?" Kane asked, trying to get the conversation back on track.

"Oh, probably first thing in the morning."

"Why not now?" Caputo asked.

"He's visiting some friends at Penn State right now. He won't be back until late tonight," Trumbell answered. "Hey guys, be at my house at 9:00 a.m. and we'll get right on it, I promise you."

"It's better than Monday," Kane said, shaking the man's hand.

Trumbell directed his attention to some commotion coming from the main entrance. "Well, looky here! If it ain't the boys from the bomb squad with all their pretty toys." Trumbell laughed.

"They want this," Caputo said, holding out the grenande.

Trumbell put a hand to his mouth and let out with a whistle that was deafening. "Over here!" he yelled to bomb squad.

The two disposal officers, dressed in full armored protection, hurried over. One recognized Caputo immediately. "Whatcha got?"

Caputo showed him the grenade. "Set to go off when a locker was opened," he added.

"Must've been something pretty important in that locker," the policeman said.

Caputo paused for a moment. "Nope!" He glanced quickly at Kane, Trumbell and then back to the disposal officers. "That's just it, the damned thing was empty."

The bomb men didn't question Caputo's word. "Okay, well we'll take that off your hands."

"Be my guest."

Caputo put the explosive gently into a heavy container the two men were carrying. The policemen replaced the lid, making certain it was securely fastened.

"Anything else?" the leader asked.

Caputo smiled. "No, that'll be it for today."

Then the silent cop spoke up. "Caputo—always the smart ass."

"Barney, is that you? I didn't recognize you with all that really neat stuff you've got on!"

Barney turned to his partner. "Come on, let's get outta here before I reach in the basket and pull the pin on that thing."

Then Barney recognized the security guard. "Hey, Joe! I'd watch out who I hung around with if I were you."

"I'd watch out what I play around with, if I were you," Trumbell said, pointing to the container.

The bomb disposal men left as quickly as they had arrived.

"If you hear a loud bang, Barney, dropped the grenade." Caputo laughed.

"I take it you're not close." Kane observed.

"We went to the academy together." Caputo laughed harder. "The clumsiest guy on the force."

"I think he joined bomb disposal just to prove he wasn't as awkward as everyone thought he was," said Trumbell.

"Well, he's still here," Kane said.

"Yeah, but he's been doing this for three years and been hospitalized five times. I wouldn't trust him to carry a birthday cake to the table."

"I'm surprised he's still got all his fingers and toes." Caputo was still laughing.

"Hey! He was wearing shoes and gloves—maybe he doesn't!" Trumbell grinned.

Chapter Sixteen

Kane's whole day had been spent with Caputo. For that matter, his entire visit had been spent with the man. He thought of how good it was to have some time alone. A night watching TV in the room didn't appeal to him, but he heard a decent-sounding band playing in the lounge, when he had walked into the hotel lobby. A brew, a little food and some good music seemed to be just what the doctor ordered.

Kane smiled as he walked into the Duquesne Room. His first impression was good. The place wasn't crowded and the room looked comfortable. The people who were there looked relaxed and happy—all except for Susan Mullen, who was seated by herself at a corner table.

Kane signaled a waitress. "An Iron City for me, and give the lady in the corner another of whatever she's drinking." He pointed to Susan.

He walked to the bar and sat down. "Look's like you've had a rough day," the bartender said as he placed a napkin and beer in front of Kane.

"It's been a rough month," Kane answered, slurping a mouthful of foam from the top of the glass.

"You in town on business or pleasure?"

Kane was about to speak, but someone answered for him.

"He's in town on business."

The detective turned toward the voice and saw Susan standing right behind him. The experienced bartender knew it was time to clean some glasses at the other end of the counter.

"Thank you for the drink," she continued. "It really wasn't necessary."

"I know," Kane said. "I saw you when I came in and you looked like you had the weight of the world on you shoulders. I figured you could use it."

Then he realized the lady was still standing. "Oh, uh, please—have a seat."

"Better yet, why don't *you* join *me*?" she said. "It's not as noisy and much more comfortable."

That was all the persuasion Kane needed. He followed the attractive young woman to her table and the couple sat down. Kane watched Susan take a sip of her wine. He laughed.

"What's funny?" she asked, somewhat defensively.

"Oh, you do that—like a lady," he answered.

"Do what?"

"You drink like a lady."

"How does a *lady* drink?"

"No big gulps. Just a measured, dignified sip."

"That sounds a bit chauvinist."

"I don't mean it to be an insult, Miss Mullen."

"You know my name!" She was genuinely surprised.

"Yes. I'm a detective and—"

"You're following me?"

"No Ma'm. I'm in town working on another case. You were pointed out to me by a detective friend of mine when we saw you and your father check in today."

Susan grinned. "Yes, well I saw you and Detective Caputo too, Mr. Kane."

Now Kane looked surprised.

Susan continued, "I had our security check you two out. It wasn't hard to do. Just about everyone in Pittsburgh knows your handsome sidekick."

"And the guy works undercover! Do you believe that?" Kane said.

"What's a retired New York detective doing—"

Kane finished, "In a place like this? I'm trying to catch a murderer."

"Any luck?"

Kane shrugged his shoulders. "I don't know. The more I investigate—the deeper I get—the more I think I'm working on a different case altogether."

Susan took another sip of her drink.

"It's personal, isn't it?"

"What do you mean?" Kane asked.

"The murder case that brought you here. The victim was a friend of yours, wasn't he?"

"Yes, Miss Mullen, he was."

"That's very admirable of you, Detective. Most people today don't put themselves out for their living friends, never mind their dead ones." She sat back in her chair. "How long have you known Detective Caputo?"

"Let's see." Kane thought for a moment. "About two days."

The young woman seemed amused. "So you're old friends."

"You may laugh, but it seems like I've known him all my life. The kid's a tough guy, and a real good cop. He's the kinda person you want covering your backside. When I was on the force, he would've been a perfect partner."

Kane took a pretzel from a bowl at the table. "How about you?" he continued. "Why are you so pensive tonight?"

A worried look came across Susan's face.

"I'm very concerned for my father."

"Why?"

"Some people want him dead."

"For what?"

"Because he's doing what you're doing."

"What do you mean?"

"My dad was an aide to President Kennedy. He had just graduated from Harvard. Kennedy, who was a senator at the time, heard my dad talk on a radio debate and was impressed by what he said and how he said it. He hired my dad as a speech writer. In a relatively short time, they became good friends—I mean *good* friends. The President trusted my dad with a lot of private stuff—things to this day he never talks about, even to me."

She paused for a moment, gathering her thoughts."When the President was killed, my father vowed he'd find the people responsible for his friend's death."

"I take it, he doesn't believe that Lee Harvey Oswald acted alone."

"Oswald! The man was a pawn. My dad said he couldn't hit the broad side of a barn door with an Uzi, never mind fire three rounds into the presidential motorcade from that distance and hit what he was aiming at."

Kane took another pretzel. "I have to agree with your dad. I never believed the story the government crammed down the public's throat. The Warren Commission was a joke. If I investigated a regular old run-of-the-mill murder the way those jerks ran that investigation, I'd have been run out of the department a long time ago."

The young woman looked out the window and then back at Kane. "Detective Kane, I asked my father not to take this trip to Pittsburgh. I begged him to postpone it until after the hearings started."

She placed the wine glass on the table, clasped her hands together and leaned closer to Kane. "I know I sound like a hysterical woman, but I'm sure someone's going to try to hurt my dad while he's in this city. It's the last good opportunity they'll have to get at him."

"Have you told the police how you feel?"

"Of course, but they don't believe me. Hell, my father thinks I'm overreacting. The authorities asked him his opinion, and he told them not to worry. He said, everything's under control. Mr. Kane, call me whatever you like, but I'm certain my dad's in danger."

"If what you say is true, I can't image the police taking your concerns lightly!"

"Detective Lauder seems like a nice man, but he's—"

Kane sat up in the chair. "Who?"

"Detective Lauder. He's the man responsible for my father's security, while he's in town."

"When was the last time you talked to him?" Kane asked.

"Well, actually, we've never met. I told him how I felt in a telephone conversation a couple of days ago."

"You may never meet him," Kane said.

"What do you mean?" she asked.

"There's a good possibility that our friend, Detective Robert Lauder, was working for the other side."

"He's a bad cop?" she asked.

"Caputo and I think so."

"Well, let's go talk to the bastard," she said, getting up from her chair, quickly.

Kane took hold of her wrist and pulled her gently back into her seat."I admire your Irish spirit, Miss Mullen. It looks good on you. The fact is, Lauder won't be double-crossing anybody anymore."

Susan eyes were filled with questions. "You killed him?" she asked.

"No, no. We think the bad guys did that."

"When?"

"Very early this morning." Kane sipped his beer. "That's probably why the good detective didn't greet you, when you arrived. He's too preoccupied explaining his actions to God."

Susan took her wine glass. "I don't like to see anybody hurt, never mind killed." She raised her drink, in a toast. "But if the son of a bitch was going kill my dad, may he burn in hell." She took a generous mouthful of wine.

Kane smiled and suddenly, at that moment, felt an emptiness. It was then that he realized he was attracted to this beautiful young woman. He imagined holding her in his arms and her face looking up at him, filled with love. Sitting across the table was the woman of his dreams. The sad, empty feeling came with the realization that it was a relationship that would go unfulfilled. He was twenty-five years her senior. The best years of her life were yet to come. The best years of his were but a memory.

"Mr. Kane. Mr. Kane!"

Her voice startled him from the daydream.

"Life's a bitch," he said somberly and took another drink.

She thought the remark was a response to her toast.

"Excuse me for being so—so vindictive. When people try to hurt my loved ones, I sometimes respond in ways that even surprise me," she said apologetically.

"Oh, I don't blame you," Kane said softly. He paused and then continued, "Do me a favor."

"Sure," she answered.

"Don't call me Mr. Kane. It makes me feel like your grandfather. Please, call me Jack."

"Of course." She reached into her purse, took out two small pieces of paper and handed them to the detective.

"What's this?" he asked.

"They're passes for tomorrow's game. They're to our booth. I'd feel much better if you and Mr. Caputo, could join us."

Kane took the tickets and slipped them into his coat pocket. "Count on us being there, Susan."

"I hate to interrupt!"

Kane looked up and, to his surprise, saw Caputo standing no more than five feet away.

"Don't you ever sleep?" Kane asked.

The wrinkled clothes and heavy growth of beard were evidence that Caputo hadn't been home yet.

"The way things are going, I may never see my bed again," Caputo said, sounding tired. Then he looked at Susan. "Miss Mullen, good to see you again. I'm—"

"Detective Caputo—I know. I feel like we're old friends. Se smiled. "Won't you join us?"

"I wish I could, he replied. "The fact is, something's come up Jack, and I think you'll want to go with me."

Kane could tell by the tone of his voice that the something was extremely important. He got up from his chair, immediately.

"It's been good talking with you, Susan. Try not to worry about your father. We'll do whatever we can." He shook her hand.

"Thank you Jack. I know you will."

The two men didn't say another word until they left the lounge and were in the lobby.

"I like your taste." Caputo said, referring to Susan.

"It was just good conversation." said Kane.

Caputo smiled. "That's always the way it starts."

"I'm old enough to be her father."

"Or at least her older brother." Caputo laughed.

They walked out of the hotel and stopped on the front sidewalk. The two men watched the stadium traffic travel the causeway toward the Fort Pitt Bridge.

"Game's over." Caputo observed.

"Ain't that the truth."

"No, I mean the Pirates game. That's where the crowd's coming from."

"Oh! I haven't been thinking much about baseball these last few days." Kane paused. "Besides, I follow the American League."

"I should've known—a Yankee fan.

Kane turned to Caputo. "What's up?"

"The river boys just pulled a floater out of the Allegheny."

"And?"

"And, it was none other than your friend and mine, Alonzo Toma."

"Well!" Kane said thoughtfully. "Hasn't been a good day for the wise guys, has it? First the creep who tried to kill me, then Lauder and now Toma!"

"And it's not even midnight yet," Caputo added. "Shall we go take a look?

"What the hell," Kane said reluctantly.

* * * *

Argari was in Toma's bedroom searching through his personal belongings when the dead man's private telephone rang. The travel alarm on the night stand next to the bed read 10:55 p.m.. He turned the volume up on the answering machine.

"Hey, you son of a bitch, if you're there, pick up."

It was Reece, and from the noise in the background, Argari guessed that he was calling from his car phone.

"I told you I'd call after the ballgame!"

Reece paused to see if Toma would answer. "Ah, you're probably taking a crap or something. I know you're there!"

Another pause. "Listen Toma, it's important we talk again and I mean *tonight.*"

Argari took a piece of paper and a pencil from a notepad next to the phone.

"I've got more to tell you about what we talked about earlier and I'm not gonna leave it on some dumb answering machine. You know where the barn is—out in South Park. Meet me there at midnight. Don't screw with me, Toma. Be there."

The phone went dead.

Argari didn't have to write much. All he had scribbled was "12 midnight" and "South Park barn." He had an hour, and he was familiar with the barn. He had bought the property and given it to Reece to use in any way he saw fit.

South Park is a rural town, about fifteen miles to the south of the city. There were no horses in Reece's barn. Argari knew that. He used the place for one purpose—as a secluded firing range. The nearest neighbor was three miles away, as the crow flies, and that was the South Hills Rod and Gun Club. No one ever complained about the gunshots. Everyone figured the reports were coming from the rifle club.

Argari summoned his two bodyguards, told them to get their weapons and then bring the car around. He ran down the hall to his room, took a coat from his closet, a loaded pistol and a spare clip from his desk drawer. Then he hurried down the stairs and out the front door to the waiting vehicle.

"You know where the barn is?" he asked the driver.

"Sure, Boss," the man replied.

"Take me there—fast," he ordered.

Argari's car raced out of the driveway and into the night.

* * * *

The medic unzipped the body bag and Caputo shined the flashlight on Toma's face.

"Not a pretty sight," said Kane.

"I'm sure he's looked better," Caputo commented.

Kane leaned in for a closer examination. "Either a very lucky shot or a very good marksman."

"I think whoever it was did what they wanted to do."

Kane stood back. "Yeah, he wasn't the sort you'd just want to nick."

Caputo turned to the attendant. "Any other wounds or marks?"

"Nope. What you see, is what he got," the man answered.

"Well, I've seen enough." Kane turned away.

"Yeah, me too." Caputo signaled for the bag to be rezipped.

The two men walked to the end of the dock.

"The plot thickens," Caputo said.

"One of two people did this," Kane said leaning against a pier support.

"Argari or—? Caputo hesitated.

"Reece," Kane said.

"Well, I think I can narrow the list a bit. They figure Toma's been dead two, maybe three hours. As you know, there was a game at the stadium this evening. Reece had to be at the ballpark when Toma was making his exit."

Kane turned and looked back at the attendants placing the body in the ambulance. "How'd they find the body so fast? He could have been in the water for days before anyone found him."

Caputo nodded in agreement. "Hell, he could've been in the water forever, with nobody ever finding him. I can't tell you how many poor souls have disappeared for good in the murky waters of these three rivers. There's a lotta crap down there—twigs, branches, trees, driftwood, old barges, sunken boats—you name it, believe me, it's there. You get stuck in it, and you're fish food."

Caputo pointed to the yacht club just up river. "Seems some people were having drinks on their houseboat when they heard a thud."

"A thud?"

"The current moves fast around here. When Toma's head hit the back of the fiberglass boat, they thought a log or some driftwood smashed into it. I mean, the asshole *did* have a big head."

"True. Needless to say, they were surprised, at what they found," Kane said.

"That's an understatement. The boat owner reached down to grab what he thought was driftwood and pulled up that mess instead. The guys said the woman on board screamed for a good fifteen minutes without taking a breath."

"I don't blame her. Sounds like a scene from a *Friday the 13th* movie."

"That Toma was always one to crash a party."

"Well, it looks like we should take a little ride over to Argari's, for a late night chat."

"Who needs sleep anyway?" Caputo said.

Chapter Seventeen

Argari had his driver switch off the headlights as they turned onto the long dirt roadway that led to the barn. About two hundred yards from the building, Argari signaled the man to stop the car and shut off the engine.

"Listen, I believe our Mr. Reece has gotten too big for his britches." He took the pistol from his coat and checked once again to make certain it was loaded. "My gut feeling tells me he was working with Toma."

The two bodyguards had been quiet all trip. As they listened to their leader in the dark car one reached for a cigarette, but Argari grabbed his lighter before the man could flick it.

"Why don't you just send up a flare, Luigi?" Argari said sarcastically.

"I'm sorry, Boss. I wasn't thinking."

"That's your problem. You never think," Arturo added.

"Enough!" Argari said, raising his hands. "We've work to do. You both have been here before. You know the layout of the building. There are two entrances—a front door—that's the one I'm going in—and a small one in the back, down at the other end of the firing range. That's the one I want you two to come in."

Arturo, the smarter of the two henchmen, seemed concerned. "Mr. Argari, you're taking a big chance. Reece is the devil himself. If you're right about him, he might shoot you as soon as he sees you."

"This must be timed perfectly. I figure it's gonna take you two about a minute to get around to the back of the building. When I think you're there, that's when I'm gonna make my move. All I want to do is distract him for a few seconds—

just long enough for you gentlemen to make your entrance. When you're inside, you pop him."

Argari leaned forward. "But—and I emphasize this strongly—make sure I'm out of the line of fire. I want you to shoot him, not me."

"How are you gonna distract him?" Luigi asked.

Argari leaned back. "I'm gonna ask him why he killed Toma."

"But he didn't kill Toma! You did," Luigi quickly responded.

Arturo shoved his companion. "You asshole! We know that. It's to make Reece stop and think for a second—to throw him off balance. It'll be long enough for us to take him out."

"Oh! Yeah, of course," Luigi said sheepishly.

Argari looked down at his watch and pressed a small button that illuminated the face. "It's almost midnight. We mustn't keep him waiting." He looked back at his men. "You know what to do, so do it."

The car's front doors opened simultaneously, and the inside overhead light came on. Argari smashed it instantly with the butt of his pistol. Arturo and Luigi stepped from the car.

"Leave the doors open," Argari ordered in a loud whisper. "He might hear them close."

The men did as they were told, turned and hurried off into the woods, weapons at the ready. Argari looked at his watch again.

* * * *

"Midnight! The bewitching hour," Reece said as he moved his watch around to catch as much moonlight as possible so he could see the time. "Argari, you sly old son of a bitch! I knew it was you as soon as I saw your friends get out of the car."

Arturo and Luigi had no idea that Reece was waiting for them in the woods just behind the barn. They moved with confidence in the darkness. About fifty yards from the back door, they did what Reece knew they would do. They decided to improvise.

Arturo turned to Luigi. "No need for the two of us to walk in at the same time. You go in first; I'll wait about a minute and follow you. This way, I can cover your back."

"Good idea," Luigi agreed.

Reece smiled as he thought, "Arturo, you're just smart enough to be dangerous."

Luigi was a big man. Reece watched him move and was amazed at how quiet he could be in the dark and on unfamiliar terrain.

"You must've been a hell of a Boy Scout, Luigi," Reece whispered, as he stepped out of the underbrush and grabbed him from behind. Reece covered Luigi's mouth with his left hand and plunged the blade of the large hunting knife under his victim's sternum, pushing it in to the hilt and then twisting it violently. Reece felt the victim stiffen and then go limp in his arms. He lowered him to the ground gently and then stepped back into the darkness. Thirty seconds later, Arturo, walking the same path stumbled over Luigi's body and fell to the ground. In the darkness, he thought he had tripped on a log or large rock.

"Damn!" he said, wiping the dirt and leaves from his clothes. He reached out to feel what it was he had fallen over and felt a warm, thick liquid.

"What the hell?" he said as he took his penlight out and examined the blood on his hands. Then he aimed the beam in Luigi's face.

"Oh, my God!" he said as he jumped back in shock.

"Yes?" Reece said cheerfully.

He panned the light to the left and, for the last second of his life, saw the blade of Reece's knife racing toward his throat. It happened too quickly for there to be any reaction. Reece slammed the knife in under Arturo's Adam's apple, at an upward angle. The eight-inch blade ripped through to Arturo's brain. Again, he concluded the act with a violent twist of the knife, meant to scramble everything. He withdrew the blade and, this time, let the body drop hard to the ground.

"Shit! This is too easy," he said, as he rammed the blade into the ground, wiping away any excess blood and gray matter. He slid the weapon into its scabbard and turned his attention to the barn.

"*Now* who's gonna be surprised?" he mumbled as he walked toward the building.

* * * *

Argari hadn't been in the barn since he purchased the property years earlier. He was astonished at the changes Reece had made. It was more than a simple target range. The barn was a shrine to all the evil things that Reece had done. Every hit—every assassination he had ever performed had a designated spot on the wall, where a framed newspaper clipping describing the event hung in tribute. Beneath each frame was a behind-the-scenes description, penned by Reece himself, of what really happened and who the people were that commissioned the act. It was the museum of a madman.

"Reece, you're out of your mind," Argari said to what he thought was an empty room.

"You don't like my Hall of Fame?" Reece stepped from behind the targets at the far end of the building. "Why, I thought you'd be crazy about it!"

The barn was lit by a handful of hanging bulbs. It was easy for Argari to step back into a dark area.

"What? Are we playing hide and seek now?" Reece asked as he continued to walk toward Argari. "Hey, what the hell's the problem?"

Argari voice was threatening. "I'd stop right there, if I were you."

Reece heard Argari pull the hammer back on the pistol, and he stopped dead in his tracks.

"Luigi! Arturo!" Argari yelled. Of course there was no response. "Luigi!Arturo!" he screamed louder this time. Still nothing.

"So, you've killed them, too. You'll need two more frames, won't you?"

"What are you talking about? They're right behind you." Reece laughed.

It was the oldest trick in the book and Argari had fallen for it. He turned, instinctively to see if the two men were there, and when he realized he'd been duped he turned back just as fast—only Reece was gone. Argari fired a wild shot into the darkness near where Reece had been standing. Suddenly, Argari felt something he hadn't felt in years—fear.

"What are you doing, Johnny? We were friends. I taught you everything you know."

"I have my orders," Reece said from a different area of the barn.

This time Argari fired two shots. Suddenly, all the lights went out. Argari froze, listening for the faintest sound that might give away his adversary's location. The silence was deafening. He crouched down and moved behind a small desk.

"Whose orders?" he yelled. "Toma's? He's dead. He can't pay you."

"I would never trust Toma," Reece said in a loud but calm voice.

Argari's eyes darted back and forth, hoping to catch a glimpse of Reece—something, anything. All there was to see was darkness. Suddenly, he realized something was missing from his pocket. The extra gun clip! It must have fallen out in all the excitement.

"Damn!" he said to himself, slapping his leg in anger at the same time. He peered around the corner of the desk.

"Well then who *is* paying you?" he yelled again.

"Let's just say, management thinks you've lost it. You're not a major leaguer any more." Reece laughed. "They sent you back to Triple A. You couldn't cut it so now they've decided not to renew your contract. It's really as simple as that."

Reece was about to make his move when he heard the hinge on the front door squeak. "You're better at this than I thought, old man!"

The killer ran to the door and pulled it open. Argari had anticipated it, stopped, turned and fired in Reece's direction. The bullet sailed past his head and landed in the wall at the opposite end of the building. Reece slammed the door closed.

"You bastard!" he said angrily. "You wanna play rough? I can play rough."

He hurried to a footlocker, lifted the cover and picked up an Uzi machine gun. The room was completely dark so he used his hands to make certain it was fully loaded and operational. He had taught himself to take his guns apart and reassemble them blindfolded. Many people could do that with one type of weapon, but few could match the variety and speed of Reece. Satisfied that it was ready, he ran back to the door and kicked it open.

Argari turned the car ignition and switched on the headlights. The high beams were just bright enough to catch the figure of Reece standing in the doorway. He dropped the shifter into drive, turned the wheel all the way to the left and pressed the gas pedal to the floor. He had just begun to make a tight U turn, when Reece fired a long and accurate burst.

"Oh shit!" Argari screamed, as the bullets pierced the car doors and shattered all the windows. Somehow, to his amazement, the engine continued to perform.

"I ain't dead yet, you son of a bitch," Argari yelled, just before Reece squeezed the trigger again. More glass disintegrated. He could hear the metal pop as the bullets tore into the car body. And then he felt a white-hot pain in his right shoulder. It happened quickly. He put his left hand to the spot where he'd felt the pain and his middle finger slipped into the wound.

"Oh man!" There was panic in his voice. "It went right through me!"

He looked into the rearview mirror—the only piece of glass on the car that wasn't broken—and could see that he was out of range.

"You're dead, you weasel!" Argari screamed as loud as he could. "You're dead!"

His hand and his shirt were now covered with blood, but his rage kept him from slipping into shock.

"You're dead, Reece, you hear me?" he yelled, viciously, as he gripped the wheel with his right hand and, with his left, stuffed his handkerchief, into the wound.

The car was almost out of sight, but Reece had heard him.

Chapter Eighteen

Kane and Caputo were drained. Both men had hoped to be sleeping in a clean bed at ten minutes past one in the morning. Instead, after waiting half an hour for a warrant to be delivered, they were rummaging through Argari's house. Caputo was doing the physical search and Kane was interviewing the only person on the premises, Argari's butler Francesco Marcone. He was a stately looking gentleman in his mid-seventies, but he looked much younger than his years. He had an honest demeanor that seemed out of place in the home of this lifelong criminal.

Kane had known Marcone for years. He realized that the secret to the man's longevity was his feigned ignorance. He never let on that he knew what the gangster's business dealings were all about. Of course, it wasn't true. You couldn't live in a building with a man like Argari, for twenty-seven years, and not know everything. Although Kane despised Argari, he actually liked Marcone.

"Francesco, we really hate to get you out of bed at this hour of the morning," he said apologetically.

Francesco tightened the belt on his robe. "And I've got to be at six o'clock mass in the morning, Detective Kane. Anything you could do to expedite these proceedings would be deeply appreciated."

Kane smiled. A hoodlum's manservant and he's concerned about getting to church on time.

"Six o'clock! Why so early, Francesco?"

"I have to be back to make breakfast for Mr. Argari and Mr. Toma."

Kane put his arm on Marcone's shoulder. "I'm afraid Mr. Toma's on a bit of a diet."

"Oh?"

Kane cleared his throat. "A police boat fished his body out of the river last night. Someone blew half his head off and then tossed him into the drink."

Then Marcone remembered the dark red stain on Mr. Argari's office carpet. Arturo and Luigi had asked him to try using some extra strength cleaner to see if he'd have better luck removing the spot. It took him two-and-a-half hours, but he did what he was asked. Good domestics always do. He figured something violent had happened there, but he didn't want to know the details. What he didn't know, he couldn't tell authorities when placed in an awkward situation, such as the one he was in at the present time.

"Oh! Dear me!" he said politely. "Well, I'm sorry to hear that. I'm sure Mr. Argari will be, too."

"We think he already knows. That's why we're here," Kane said.

Francesco walked to a high-back chair and sat down. "Excuse me for asking, Detective Kane. Are you a member of the Pittsburgh Police department now?"

"Nope. I'm simply an observer on this one, Francesco."

"I see."

"That's why Detective Caputo's performing the search and not me."

Marcone understood. "I see. He has jurisdiction and you don't."

"I'm just along for the ride."

The old man smiled. "Some ride, huh, Detective? You look like you haven't slept in days."

Kane nodded. "I can think of a hundred places I'd rather be, right now."

He walked to a window, looked out and then turned back to Marcone. "Can you tell us anything, Francesco?"

"What do you mean, Sir?"

"Do you know who shot Toma? Do you know where Argari is now?"

"I'm afraid I can't help you with either question, Detective. Saturday I was off, and I was gone most of the day. I just returned a couple of hours ago," he lied.

"Francesco, if you're not telling the truth, I'd suggest abstaining from communion at mass tomorrow. God won't be happy."

Francesco lowered his eyes. "I'll remember that, Detective Kane."

Caputo appeared at the top of the stairs. "Hey, Jack!" he started down the staircase. "I looked everywhere, but the only thing I could find was this."

Kane could see that he was holding a small piece of paper. They met at the bottom of the stairs.

"Obviously, he took the note with him. He left this indentation on the pad. I shaded the page with a lead pencil and was able to bring this out." He seemed proud. "Some things they teach you in Boy Scouts you never forget."

Kane took the paper and read it out loud, "Twelve midnight—South Park barn." He looked at his watch and then handed the paper back to Caputo. "Whatever happened at this barn, happened an hour-and-a-half ago—and that's assuming that note was written last night. For all we know, it could be two months old."

Kane turned to Marcone, who was still sitting quietly in the chair. "Francesco, you know of some barn in—" he looked back at Caputo. "What was the name of that place?"

"South Park." he replied.

"Yeah, right." He asked the question again. "You know of some barn in South Park?"

Marcone thought for a moment. "I'm sorry, gentlemen, I'm afraid I don't know of any barn in South Park or anywhere else."

Kane studied Marcone's face. "I don't know about you, Francesco."

Then Kane remembered a possibility. "Hey, Caputo, did Toma have an answering machine?"

"Yeah, and I checked it. It's one of those new ones that erases the messages once you've listened to them. The tape was blank."

"Well, if you're all done, why don't we call it a night." Kane rubbed his eyes. "We've got an early call in the morning."

"Marcone, I'm leaving a car out front to greet Mr. Argari when he comes home. If he calls, tell him we want to talk with him, immediately. Here's my number." Caputo handed a card to the servant. "Call any time, day or night. Thank you for your help."

The two men started to leave. Caputo was the first out the door, but Kane stopped and turned back to Marcone. "Francesco, if I were you, I'd hit confession before mass tomorrow."

Kane stepped outside and pulled the door shut.

Marcone looked at the card, took a deep sigh, put his head back in the chair and closed his eyes.

* * * *

Argari found it difficult to hold the binoculars steady with his one good hand. He had parked on a service road that ran along the side of his property. From his vantage point, he could see the uninvited guests at his house. He watched Kane and Caputo leave. He noticed the cruiser take position in front of the main gate. He saw Marcone come out the kitchen door at the back of the house and walk into the darkness.

Argari put the binoculars on the seat and looked down at his wound. There was blood everywhere.

"I have bandages and some pain killers, Mr. Argari."

Argari looked back quickly. "You startled me, Francesco." He put his head against the headrest and closed his eyes for a moment. "I'm glad I was able to reach you before the Lone Ranger and Tonto showed up. Thank God Reece didn't shoot the car phone."

The servant flashed his penlight on the hole in Argari's shoulder. "You know, Sir, you need medical attention right now."

"I haven't got time. I've got too many things to do."

Marcone walked around to the passenger side, opened the door, wiped a great deal of glass from the seat and got it. "The problem is, there's a good possibility you won't live to do those things if you don't see a doctor."

"Francesco, weren't you a medic in the war?"

"Yes, Sir, but that was a long, long time ago."

"You haven't lost your touch, my friend."

Marcone looked exasperated. "You need blood and you need antibiotics. I don't have access to either. All I can do is bandage you up and give you aspirin!"

"That'll do just fine," Argari said. "The bullet went through, right?"

Marcone was staring into the wound. "You've got a hole through you the size of the Fort Pitt Tunnel," he answered. "I'll patch you up Sir, but if you don't get help, you're gonna die."

Argari turned, wild-eyed, to Marcone. "I'm not gonna die! Not until I kill that ungrateful son of a bitch, Reece. After that, I don't care."

"Sir! You can't mean that."

Argari clutched at his aching shoulder. "I mean every word. Now, get to work," he ordered.

Good servant that he was, Marcone did as he was told and, considering the conditions, dressed the wound nicely. Then he returned to the house, put together a change of clothes and hurried back to Argari.

"Good man, Francesco. Did anybody see you?"

"No. There's only that one car out front, and I think he's asleep," he answered as he handed him the items. "Sir, my car is parked at the end of the service road, as usual."

He reached into his pocket, took out some car keys and put them on the dashboard.

"Thank you, my friend," Argari said. "This car barely made it here. I've seen Swiss cheese with fewer holes." Argari grinned painfully. "Now get outta here. I'll rest here a few hours and then go about my business."

Marcone started to climb out of the car but Argari grabbed his hand. "Francesco, have some money—quite a bit of money—in a security box that's beneath a false bottom, under the lower right-hand drawer of my desk." He slipped a small key into Marcone's hand. "I want you to take it, and I want you to leave first thing in the morning."

"But sir!"

"Please, Francesco, do as you're told." He paused. "Call it your retirement fund—call it your severance pay, I don't care. It's for your own good."

I don't need your money, Sir. You've been very generous over the years and I've been able to save."

"If you don't take it, Francesco, the government's going to confiscate it. The idea of them seizing four hundred thousand dollars of my money hurts me a hell of a lot more than this bullet hole."

Now Marcone was the one who appeared to be in shock. "Four hundred thousand dollars! Sir, I can't take all your money."

Argari laughed. "Francesco, I'm not giving you *all* my money—just the loose change in the study. Please! I'm tired. Go, my friend, and enjoy the remaining years of your life."

"I'll miss you, sir."

"And I you, Francesco. Go."

"Very well, Sir," Marcone said somberly.

Argari glanced at a car that passed by the main entrance, and when he looked back to Marcone, he was gone.

"That's what I always liked about you, Francesco. You were perfect at making a discreet exit."

He set the alarm on his watch for seven, leaned against the door, closed his eyes and fell asleep quickly.

Chapter Nineteen

Kane looked over Ronny Trumbell's shoulder and watched as the young man put the computer through its paces. Joe Trumbell was in the kitchen making coffee, and Caputo was in the next room talking to headquarters. Kane seemed to be amazed at the different things the device appeared to be doing.

"Mr. Kane, accessing this is real easy," Ronny said. "You've got a couple of different things on this disk."

"A couple! With all that different stuff popping up on the screen, it looks like you've got the *Encyclopedia Britannica* in there."

The polite young man laughed. "No, it's not as complicated as all that."

He pressed a few buttons and the screen filled with numbers. "This is from a spreadsheet file. This type of file ties into an accounting program."

He punched some keys and the screen changed again. This time the text from a letter appeared. "And this file works with a word processing program," Ronny continued.

"Can you print it—you know, give me a hard copy?" Kane asked.

"Well, I'm not sure what programs they actually work with, but.—" He punched the keyboard again and smiled. "Yeah, I can do this. It's a piece of cake. It's just gonna take me a little time."

Kane looked at his watch. They had already been at Trumbell's house for two hours. "Take whatever time you need." Kane put his hand on Ronny's shoulder. "But, please, do it as fast as you can, okay?"

"Mr. Kane, I'll put this thing into overdrive," Ronny said, tapping the top of his monitor.

"Thanks Ronny."

Kane turned and went into the next room to talk with Caputo. As he entered, Caputo hung up the phone.

"That kid's incredible." Kane gestured in the direction of Ronny.

Caputo smiled and turned toward Kane. "This case is like a damned roller coaster ride, except, it won't stop to let you off!"

Kane pulled up a chair and sat down. "Now what?"

"You know why I was on the phone so long?"

"I don't know? Maybe you got a girlfriend at headquarters," Kane answered.

"I wish," Caputo said. "Headquarters was giving me the details on a barn fire out in South Park."

"How'd they get that information? I mean, who knew to send that along to the Pittsburgh Police?"

"When I got home this morning, I called in; told them about the note we found at Argari's. I asked them to keep an eye out for anything that might tie into all this." Kane waved his hand like he was telling traffic to come forward.

"And? Don't keep me in suspense."

Caputo looked down at the notebook pad he was holding. "County police notified us of a major barn fire." He looked up and smiled. "And I don't mean the kind you find at pep rallies either" He looked back at his notes and continued, "A major barn fire at a very secluded location, just off Route 88 in South Park."

"Might be a coincidence." Kane said.

"Normally, I'd think the same thing, if not for the fact that they found two crispy critters in the middle of the smoking embers."

"So?" Kane was unconvinced.

"These poor souls didn't die from the fire. They were dead before it started. Both were knifed."

Kane leaned forward in the chair. "Hmm, fascinating."

"Wait! The best is yet to come. Guess who owns the barn?"

"I don't know! Donald Trump?" Kane sat back.

"Even better than that." He tapped the point of his pencil on the notebook pad. "Would you believe the owner of record is our friend Argari?"

"The guy's everywhere! Any idea who the victims are?" Kane asked.

"They've got a pretty good idea," Caputo said.

"Those lab boys are great, aren't they?"

"Lab boys, my ass! A uniformed county cop found a wallet in the woods out back. It belonged to one of Argari's men. I figure he went there to do business and the deal went bad. They also found a trail of blood leading to the barn."

"You think the other one was Argari?" Kane asked.

"I don't think so. Both bodies were over six feet tall. Argari's five-eight," Caputo continued, "He had two personal bodyguards."

"Right. Arturo and Luigi," Kane said.

"Well then, you also know they went everywhere with him."

"When I was on the force, back in New York, the guys used to say that whenever Argari went to the bathroom, Arturo handed him the paper and Luigi wiped," Kane said.

"Charming! Caputo wrinkled his nose. "Oh, and by the way, both men were over six feet tall.

"Sounds like their guarding days are over."

Joe Trumbell entered the room carrying three cups of coffee on a small tray. "Some people have compared my coffee to motor oil," he said as he handed a cup to each man. "I resent that. Transmission fluid, maybe, but motor oil, no way."

The three men laughed and took a sip. Suddenly, Ronny rushed into the room. "Mr. Kane! I got what you wanted!" He smiled. "And I think you're gonna like it."

"Way to go Ronny!" he said, as if cheering for a high school athlete.

Kane was the first out of the room. As Caputo walked by Trumbell, he stopped and put his coffee cup on the tray. "Joe, I said it before and I'll say it again—it tastes like motor oil." He smiled and walked into the other room.

"No way," Trumbell said defensively. Then he took a sip. "Well, maybe." He put the tray down and followed the other men.

The high school senior handed a stack of computer paper to Kane. "This is everything," the younger Trumbell said.

"It'll take hours to read!"

Kane split the stack and handed half to Caputo. Caputo thumbed through his.

"Oh good. I get the boring spreadsheets. You're looking at a guy who got Cs in math," he said as he looked at the papers Kane was holding. "You get the diary. It's not fair."

Kane grinned. "Just the luck of the Irish, my friend. Besides, I flunked math. Why don't we find ourselves a comfortable place to work, and get started."

His comfortable place was a recliner in the corner. Caputo spread his material out on the dining room table.

"I'll make some more coffee." Joe Trumbell offered.

Kane and Caputo responded quickly and in unison, "No thank you!"

* * * *

Reece pulled his Hummer into his assigned stadium parking space and turned off the ignition. He reached over the front seat and raised the tarp that covered the weapons and munitions he had taken from the barn before setting it on fire.

"Look at all these toys!" he said.

He reached behind a small wooden box filled with hand grenades—the kind used by the US Army—retrieved a .45 caliber pistol and slapped a full clip into the handgrip. "When you talk, my sweet, everybody listens," Reece said as he pulled back the breech on the pistol and a round snapped into the chamber.

On his most important assignments, the .45 was his weapon of choice. Most of his competitors would question using a gun that was as bulky and inaccurate as the Colt; but Reece felt that from fifteen feet in no other hand weapon was a deadly. The trick was going to be getting within fifteen feet of the senator.

Reece slid the pistol into his gym bag and zipped it shut. The killer smiled. He knew getting close would be simple. The VIP box wasn't much wider than fifteen feet. He pulled the canvas back and tucked in the corner. Reece then performed a quick visual inspection to make sure no one could see any part of the arsenal he was carrying. Satisfied that everything was secure, he took his gym bag, stepped out of the car, pressed the switch that locked all the doors and closed the driver's side.

"Johnny Reece!" yelled a man's voice.

The ballplayer spun around, ready for the worst.

"You're Johnny Reece, right?"

It was a fan. An overweight young man in his early twenties who had been told by someone that if he waited by Reece's parking space, he could probably get an autograph.

"Yeah, right," Reece said, trying to get his heart to slow down.

"Would you mind giving me your autograph?" the fan asked as he held out a baseball covered with signatures from other ballplayers. "I've been waiting here since six o'clock this morning. You're my favorite pitcher, Johnny."

"Six o'clock!" Reece looked at his watch. It was twelve-thirty. "You've been here for six- and-a-half hours?"

"Yup," the man said proudly.

"What a jerk," Reece thought.

He took the ball, walked to the player's entrance and stopped.

"You want my autograph, huh?"

Reece leaned back and, with the rocking motion and effort of a centerfielder trying to throw somebody out at home plate, threw the fan's baseball into the causeway that wraps around the stadium. The ball bounced once before it was hammered by a fast-moving tractor-trailer that sent it flying into Roberto Clemente Park.

The fan looked up at Reece in disbelief.

"I don't do autographs," he said with a mean smile. Then he disappeared behind the door marked "No Admittance—Pirate Personnel Only."

The fan stood staring at the door for a moment, trying to absorb what had just happened. Then the expression on his face changed to one of anger. Reece had failed to notice that the fan had an autographed baseball bat in his other hand. The man walked to the Hummer, and with one powerful swat, smashed the rear window on the passenger side and hurried away, satisfied with his revenge.

"Good for you." Argari laughed, as he watched the man run down the street. He sat slouched down behind the steering wheel of Francesco's Escort that he had parked one row up and seven cars down from the Jeep. He put his hand to his damp bandage. The white gauze was now all red. He leaned against the headrest and closed his eyes. He'd need some time to rest in order to garner strength for his next move. He knew he was dying, but it would have to wait until he finished dealing with Reece.

* * * *

Kane walked over to Caputo, dropped the computer paper on the dinning room table and pointed to an entry. "Look at this! It's Toma's insurance policy. What we've got here is a diary that describes everything Argari's been up to, blow by blow, for the past five years. The damned thing's amazing!" Kane said. "And guess what?"

Caputo didn't hesitate. "Reece is Argari's own personal hit man."

Kane looked surprised. "When did you figure that out?"

Caputo grabbed some of the paper he'd been reading through. "It's in the numbers, my friend—payments, receipts—everything's here. Every time Argari had Reece do a hit, Toma logged it into his computer. You were right. He had Kaplan whacked."

"By Reece?" Kane asked.

"You got it," Caputo answered. "And this—this scares the living daylights outta me." He ran his finger along a set of numbers. "It's Toma's most recent entry. The boys in Chicago want somebody taken out, and Argari's given Reece the assignment. From what I see here, they paid him big bucks to do the job—and I mean big with a capital B."

"Any idea when it's supposed to come down?" asked Kane.

"If I've got this figured out correctly, it's supposed to happen today."

Kane stepped back. "Today!" he thought a moment. "It has to be the senator."

Caputo agreed. "Great minds think alike."

Kane checked the time on the mantel clock. "It's one thirty-five! The game's already started. We'd better get there fast."

The two men started for the door just as Joe Trumbell entered the room. "Hey guys, where's the fire?"

Caputo shook his hand. "Joe, thanks for everything. We couldn't have done it without the help from you and your boy. I'll make sure downtown hears about this."

"Done what?"

But by the time the question was asked, Kane and Caputo were out the door.

Trumbell shrugged his shoulders. "Guess I better turn off the coffee."

Chapter Twenty

Susan sat in the VIP box quietly watching the ballgame with her father and his bodyguard. The other armed gentleman stood watch, just outside the entrance to their box. Unless you were a guest, no one could get by these two men. She felt more at ease now that the game had started and things seemed to be under control.

She had worried about the ride to the stadium and her father's glad-handing at the main gate. He wasn't running for re-election, but shaking hands with his public was one of the things the senator loved best about his job. Thousands of people had unsecured access to him there, and nothing bad had happened. If someone wanted him dead, the main gate would have been the perfect opportunity. Of course, an assassin could have picked him off when he threw out the baseball, just before the start of the game. And thank goodness she had been able to talk him out of the front row seats, the ball club had first offered him. It was the location he preferred and, under normal circumstances, he would have used them. Luckily, she had convinced him that these weren't normal circumstances.

"You enjoying the game, honey?" the senator asked.

Susan leaned toward her father. "Oh yes, very much. And you?"

"I'd like it better if Johnny had better stuff. The Mets are hitting him. To give up three runs in the first three innings—that's not Johnny Reece!" he said with the intensity of a true Pirates fan. "It almost looks like he's doing it on purpose."

"Hey Dad, win or lose, I'm still glad we're here." Susan looked up at the clear blue sky and then down at the capacity crowd, enjoying the warmth of a sunny day. "We couldn't have ordered better weather."

"It's a great day for a game," he said, raising his binoculars to his eyes. "For that matter, it's a great day to be alive."

Susan looked at her dad, didn't say a word and then looked back at the game. She knew that the last half of his remark was said innocently. He never believed for one minute that his life was in danger. The way the day was developing, he was probably right.

Caputo adjusted the volume on the car radio. "Well, as long as he's in the game, we know everything's okay. He can't shoot anybody when he's on the mound."

Kane pounded his hand against the dashboard. "A traffic jam on a Sunday! And look at this! We're trapped on the middle of a rusty old bridge. This is ridiculous! Can't these damn cars move any faster?"

"Relax Jack. This is Pittsburgh. They're always messing around with a road somewhere, no matter the day of the week. And this rusty old bridge, known to the natives as the West End Bridge, has just gone through a two-year renovation. I guarantee you it's in better shape than your George Washington Bridge. Now, there's the stadium." Caputo pointed to his right. "We're about five minutes away. They're rotating traffic, so we'll be moving soon. Take it easy. Everything's under control."

Just then, the Pirate's play-by-play announcer Lanny Frattare changed the tone of his voice. Kane leaned toward the speaker and motioned for Caputo to be quiet. "The Pirate manager is walking toward the mound," Frattare said, in his dramatic announcing style. "He hasn't signaled a change just yet. Looks like he wants to talk to Reece before he makes his decision."

* * * *

Reece took off his cap and wiped the sweat from his brow. The manager and catcher arrived at the mound at the same time.

"Hey Johnny, what the hell are you doing?" the catcher asked. "You're not throwing anything I call! I signal curve, you throw change up. I ask for a knuckle ball and you throw inside. They're hitting you like it's batting practice!"

"Hey, I'm not doing it intentionally," Reece lied.

The manager stepped between them. "Both of you shut up. We've got a game to play here." He turned to Reece and said, "Now, what's the matter? You feeling okay?"

"To be honest with you, Coach, I feel like shit." Reece wiped his brow again. "I think I have the flu or something."

The manager turned immediately to the bullpen in right field and tapped his right arm.

* * * *

"Looks like that's all for Johnny Reece," Frattare said. "They're calling for a right-hander. I can see there's some activity down there, but I can't tell you just yet who the new pitcher will be. There's a break in the action, with the score, the New York Mets three and the Pittsburgh Pirates nothing."

Kane switched off the radio. "Look, we can't wait for this traffic to move. Can you run?" he asked.

Caputo looked surprised. "Can *I* run? Sure! I run three miles every day, and I'm a helluva lot younger than you. The question is, at your age, can *you* run?"

"I ran around the streets of New York my whole life. Don't worry about me. How far is to the stadium, if we run?"

"Ten or fifteen minutes."

Kane pushed open the door. "Then, let's go."

"What about the car?" Caputo asked.

"Let 'em tow it. Let the city pay its own fine."

"Okay," Caputo said as he climbed out of the car.

The two men hadn't run twenty feet, when people stuck in traffic behind the empty cab, started blowing their horns, in protest. Caputo turned to his running partner. "This is not a way to make friends."

"Let's just hope we can stop a murder," Kane responded, and he ran a little faster.

* * * *

Reece walked through the dugout and down the hallway into the locker room. The trainer walked over to him.

"You want some ice on that elbow?"

Reece shook his head. He knew he was faking it and the arm was fine. "No. Maybe later," he answered. "I think I'm gonna go up and see some friends."

The trainer frowned. "Johnny, you know you're not supposed to walk around the stadium in your uniform when there's a game in progress."

"Look, I'll change my shoes," he said, kicking off his cleats. "Now I'm not wearing my whole uniform."

"You're stretching it, Johnny."

Reece put his arm on the trainer's shoulder. "Hey, Mac, it's the senator's daughter. I wanna impress her a bit. I can't do that in a three-piece suit. She sees them all the time in DC," he said, smiling. "If I walk in wearing my sweaty uniform it'll work like a charm. Besides, no one will see me. I'll use the private elevator. Heck, it stops right behind the VIP box."

The trainer considered the argument for a moment. "I don't know about you, Johnny. You're gonna get your ass in trouble, one of these days."

Reece smiled devilishly. "Not me!"

"Alright, do what you wanna do, but if you get caught, I never saw you," the trainer said.

"The locker room was empty," Reece agreed, embellishing the lie.

The trainer turned and walked up the ramp to the dugout. Now the killer really was alone. Reece flipped through the combination on his lock. It released and he pulled his locker door open. He reached into the gym bag, looked around to make certain no one was watching, took out the loaded .45 and tucked it under his belt. Then he grabbed a Pirates jacket from a hook on the back of the locker door and put it on. The coat concealed the pistol nicely.

* * * *

The private phone rang in the VIP box and the guard answered. After a moment, he placed it on the counter and walked over to the senator. "Sir, it's Johnny Reece. He says now that he's out of the game, he'd like to stop up and say hello."

The senator's face filled with excitement. "By all means, tell him to come right up. Oh, and make sure the guard at the door let's him in."

"Yes sir," the man answered and returned to the phone.

"Isn't that nice, Susan? Johnny Reece is coming up to say hello. It might be nice if you were to greet him at the door."

The senator's daughter smiled. "Is that really necessary, Dad?"

Just then, Brian Giles slapped a double into right field and the senator was back into the game.

* * * *

Caputo was surprised at the condition Kane was in. He'd expected the older detective to weaken quickly and have to stop to catch his breath. Kane wasn't even breathing heavily. The man seemed to grow stronger with each step.

"I didn't know you could run!" Caputo said as he kept pace, stride for stride.

"I've completed ten New York City marathons."

"You did? How well did you finish?"

"Let's just say, I was happy to finish the same day the races were started."

Caputo laughed as the two men rounded a corner and headed into a stadium parking lot.

* * * *

The elevator bell rang and a second later the doors opened. Reece stepped out and looked to the left. The door to the VIP box was open and Susan was standing in the hallway talking to the guard.

"Sorry to keep you waiting," he said, as he started toward them. "I had to side-step some autograph hounds."

"Nice to see you again, Mr. Reece." Susan said formally, extending her hand to Reece.

"Good to see you, too," he replied, shaking her hand vigorously. "I hope you don't mind me stopping up unexpectedly like this."

"Not at all. My father's dying to see you."

"Oh really!" He smiled as he adjusted his baseball cap.

Reece looked in and could see the senator seated at the far end of the box. The other guard was in the kitchen area, near the door, pouring some soda.

Susan motioned toward the opened door. "Shall we go in?"

"Absolutely."

Reece moved toward the box. It was all coming together now. Everything was falling into place as if it were meant to be. But suddenly, the hallway guard placed his hand on Reece's shoulder, stopping him.

"I'm sorry, Sir. I have to search you before you can go in," he said

"What?" Reece pretended to be shocked. "What do you think I'm carrying in my damn uniform—a nail file or some extra chew?"

The guard looked at Susan and then back to Reece. "I have my orders, Sir. It'll only take a minute."

"Susan, this is silly!"

The young woman appeared sympathetic. "I know, but everyone has to do it—even friends of the family. It'll just take a second."

Reece walked over and leaned up against the wall. "I suppose you wanna do it like it's done in the movies?"

The guard seemed embarrassed. "That's not necessary. If you'll just stand over here."

Reece slipped his hand into his jacket while the guard was talking, grabbed the .45 from his belt and cocked it. In the same motion, he spun around and fired into the man's chest, from point-blank range. The guard was dead before he could change the expression on his face. The man responsible for the senator's safety inside the box, slammed the door shut as soon as he heard the shot—almost as if it were a reflex action. Reece hurried to the door, but it was locked.

"Son of a bitch!" he yelled.

He turned quickly and saw Susan looking down at the dead man's body. She was motionless, overcome by shock and fear. Reece grabbed her arm and pulled her to him, as if she were a shield. He looked around, desperately. Now, everything was coming apart. He fired two wild rounds into the door, but they had no effect.

"I'm gonna kill your daughter!" he screamed in at the senator.

The senator was on the floor, behind a partition. "My God! He's got Susan!" he yelled to his guard. "We've gotta do something!"

But the aide was already on the phone to stadium security.

Reece stepped closer and fired into the lock. Part of the door disappeared, but the lock remained secure. Susan started to scream frantically, and that only made Reece more unsure. He put his free hand over her mouth and she bit into it.

"You bitch!" he screamed, as he threw her to the ground. She started to get up, but he whipped her across the face with the butt of his gun, and she slumped to the floor. He aimed the weapon at her head, but for some reason, he hesitated.

"You slut!" he yelled." I wasn't gonna kill you! Only your old man!"

Susan lay on the floor pretending to be unconscious—anticipating the end.

"Drop it, Reece." Caputo was standing thirty feet down the hallway with his gun pointed at the killer. Instead, Reece dropped to the floor, aimed and fired a round into Caputo's thigh, knocking him off his feet and sending Caputo's gun flying.

Reece got up and looked at Susan. "You're a lucky girl." He laughed, as he pointed the gun at her once more. "If I had more time, I'd use my knife on you."

He pulled the hammer back to fire, but a gun roared and a bullet narrowly missed his head. He looked to his right, where Caputo lay wounded, and saw Kane aiming to fire again.

"I knew I should've killed you when I had the chance!" he yelled, as he jumped a railing catlike, and landed on a ramp that led to the floor below. Kane fired once more, but this time the bullet hit a concrete pylon and ricocheted wildly out over the parking lot.

Caputo was trying to get to his feet, but the best he could do was to pull himself to a sitting position against the wall. Kane knelt down beside his friend.

"Get him," Caputo ordered, apparently in a great deal of pain.

"How about you?" Kane asked.

"Forget me. I'll be okay. Get that sicko, before he gets away."

Then Kane looked up and saw Susan standing next to him. "I'll see that he's taken care of, Mr. Kane," she said, kneeling down and taking Caputo's hand. "And thank you."

It was all Kane needed to hear. A moment later, was running down the ramp in search of an assassin.

* * * *

Reece had a significant head start on Kane, and the two levels below were filled with people. It was easy for him to blend in with the crowd. The gunshots had been muffled by the stadium noise. Other than some police hurrying toward a different ramp, everything else appeared normal. The odds of him getting away were increasing by the second.

Then he heard, "Reece!"

He looked up and saw Kane at the top of a crowded escalator. He knew the detective couldn't shoot at him. There were too many people in the line of fire. The killer, knowing Kane's predicament, flipped him the middle finger defiantly and disappeared around a corner.

The killer jumped another railing, but this time he twisted his ankle when he landed. He stumbled up against a wall.

"Damn it to hell!" he yelled, as he clutched his ankle.

A man reached to help him. "You alright, Mister?"

Reece responded by pushing him to the floor, as he quickly limped away.

* * * *

Kane came around the top of the ramp just as two men were helping the good Samaritan to his feet.

"Did a guy in a Pirates jacket do this to you?" Kane asked.

"Yeah. The asshole jumped that railing and twisted his ankle. I went to give him a hand and the jerk knocked me down."

"You're lucky that's all he did to you," Kane said. "Which way did he go?"

The man shook his head. "I'm not sure. When he took off, I was flat on my ass."

Another man volunteered, "I think I saw him go that way."

"Thanks," Kane said as he resumed the chase.

The witness had the best intentions, but he had pointed in the wrong direction. Unknowingly, Kane was running away from Reece. After running for two or three more minutes, and not seeing a sign of the assailant, he stopped a stadium attendant.

"Hey pal, where do the players park their cars?"

The man gave him a strange look. "What?"

"The players cars—where are they parked?"

"Who are you?"

Reece grabbed the man by the collar. "Listen! I'm chasing a murderer and I haven't got time to bullshit!" he screamed.

The man pointed over Kane's shoulder, in the opposite direction. "The other side of the stadium—lower level, between Gates A and D."

"Great!" Kane said sarcastically. He released the man and ran off.

The attendant walked to one of the security phones. "You better get some people down to the players parking lot. I think we've got a problem."

* * * *

Reece hurried out the player's entrance, stopped and looked back. He did it. He'd managed to lose Kane. He ran to his Hummer, fumbled with his keys, unlocked the driver's side door and got in. He closed the door and let out with a howl of delight. He snapped his seatbelt on and started the motor. As he was adjusting his rear view mirror, he noticed the canvas move and Argari sit up.. Reece went for his pistol, but Argari's was already drawn.

"You pull that thing out and I'll splatter your brains all over the windshield."

Reece stopped abruptly.

"Put both hands on the steering wheel where I can see them."

It was then that Reece realized how weak Argari sounded. He placed his hands on the wheel, as he was told, but turned his head far enough to see Argari's blood soaked clothes and his pale complexion.

"You don't look very good, my friend," Reece said, smiling. "As a matter of fact, I think you're gonna die, real soon."

Argari fought for the strength to hold the gun up. "First, I wanted Kane dead because he took out my brother." He gasped for air. "His death was top priority. But when you tried to kill me, you became number one on my hit list."

Argari started to shake, and a moment later his trembling hand released the pistol, and it fell to the floor.

Reece laughed, as he reached over and retrieved Argari's gun. *"Tried* to kill you? I *did* kill you. It's just taking a little time, that's all."

Argari's breathing was labored. It was an effort to keep his eyes open. "You've got a lot of shit back here," he struggled to say.

Reece laughed. "Yeah, I like to hunt. I don't think you'll be around to go with me, next trip."

Argari coughed up some blood.

"Hey man, you're bleeding all over my car." Reece smiled, looking into the rearview again, as he pulled the floor shifter into drive.

"You remember the booby trap trick I taught you and Toma—the one I learned in the war with the grenade?" Argari asked, as his limp hand pointed toward the front of the car.

Reece remembered instantly and looked down at the stick shift. When he'd put the car into gear, he had pulled the pin on a grenade Argari taped to the console. Reece thought he heard Argari laugh, as he reached for the door handle. It was much too late for an escape. Time had run out for Reece.

* * * *

Kane ran from the player's entrance, just in time to hear Reece yell, "Argari! You bastard!"

And then he saw the Hummer explode into the air, flip upside down and land on its roof, in a ball of flames. Kane dropped to the ground on the initial blast. As he started to get up, there was a subsequent explosion and he fell to the sidewalk again. After three or four minutes of silence, he crawled to a parked car and, using it as protection, peeked over the hood at the wreckage. All that remained were burning clumps of metal.

Kane stood and walked a few steps closer. He inadvertently kicked something and when he looked down. It caught his attention. He picked up the tarnished money clip and rubbed away some of the grime. The inscription spelled one word: "Argari."

Kane turned away and smiled. Reece and Argari were gone. The world would be a safer place tonight.

Epilogue

Caputo adjusted his weight in the bed. "If I had known this was gonna happen to me when I first met you at the airport, I'd have let some other cabby pick you up!"

Kane smiled. "What are you complaining about? You're surrounded by good-looking nurses."

Just then a male nurse entered the room, carrying a tray of medication. Kane shook his head.

"I stand corrected! But you're probably gonna get a promotion—maybe even a medal. And, above everything else, you're a hero."

"You're a bullshit artist."

"No, actually, I work with watercolors."

They both laughed.

"I'm gonna miss you pal," Kane said, putting his hand on Caputo's shoulder. "You've been one helluva partner."

"Hey, you're not rid of me yet. The way my luck's going, they'll nudge me off the force because of this little injury, and I'll have to become a PI, too."

"Hell, maybe we'll become partners!" Kane said.

"I don't know if I can work in New York," Caputo said.

"I don't know if I can work in Pittsburgh," Kane added.

There was silence for a second. Then Kane became serious. "You get better and we'll cross that bridge when we get to it."

"What bridge?" Caputo grinned.

"Why, the George Washington Bridge, of course." Kane smiled.

"No way! What you mean is the Fort Pitt Bridge."

Kane looked up and saw the nurse quietly signal him to leave. "Listen Caputo—now I'm being serious. When you get better, let's talk. I may offer you something you can't refuse."

Caputo's eyes widened. "I didn't know you had a sister!"

Kane took a deep breath and turned to the nurse. "Keep him in here as long as you can. It's safer for everybody."

Kane walked to the door, opened it and turned back to his friend. "Caputo."

"What?"

"Thanks."

Caputo hesitated for a moment. "For you, anytime."

"We'll be talking." Kane said.

"You know it." Caputo responded.

Kane stepped into the hall and pulled the door closed behind him. Caputo's room was on the third floor and at least a five-minute walk to the hospital lobby, but Kane was daydreaming.

By the time he snapped out of it, he was standing next to the newspaper stand at the main entrance. In front of him, the headline from the latest edition of the *Pittsburgh Post-Gazette*: "Pirates Star Reece Dies in Bombing."

"Damn shame if you ask me." Kane turned. It was the newspaper vendor.

"What do you mean?" Kane asked.

"What happened to Johnny Reece? Helluva pitcher. They say he was a terrific guy, too."

Kane stared at the man for a second and then answered. "You can't always believe what you read in the newspapers."

The detective turned and walked out of the hospital. It was raining but there was an empty cab parked in front of the building. Kane got in.

"Where to?" the driver asked.

"The airport," said Kane.

The cabby pulled away from the curb. The driver looked in his rearview mirror. "Where you from?" he asked.

"New York."

"What brings you to Pittsburgh?"

Kane paused and then grinned. "Hardware convention."

He continued to smile as he closed his eyes and leaned against the back of the seat. He could rest now. He'd worry about his next case—tomorrow.

978-0-9841160-

www.ingramcontent.com/pod-product-compliance
Lightning Source LLC
LaVergne TN
LVHW091004080826
845145LV00003B/1115

* 9 7 8 0 9 8 4 1 1 6 0 0 3 *